What the critics are saying

Gold Star Award

"…I was completely swept away by this erotic tale of lust and love… When I finished I was compelled to read it again - immediately!"

- Amber Taylor, *Just Erotic Romance Reviews*

Gold Star Award

"…I never thought that Ms. King would be able to outdo herself - and I am happy to say that I was wrong. This book is a must read irrespective of your category of preference."

- Mireya Orsini, *Just Erotic Romance Reviews*

"…With Fetish Ms. King proves once more that she is a master at powerfully erotic paranormal romance."

- Vikky Bertling, *The Road to Romance*

Discover for yourself why readers can't get enough of the multiple award-winning publisher Ellora's Cave. Whether you prefer e-books or paperbacks, be sure to visit EC on the web at www.ellorascave.com for an erotic reading experience that will leave you breathless.

www.ellorascave.com

Also by Sherri L. King:

Bachelorette

Chronicles of the Aware: Rayven's Awakening

Midnight Desires (anthology)

Moon Lust

Moon Lust: Bitten

Moon Lust: Mating Season

The Horde Wars: Ravenous

The Horde Wars: Wanton Fire

The Horde Wars: Razor's Edge

Twisted Destiny (anthology)

FETISH
An Ellora's Cave Publication, February 2004

Ellora's Cave Publishing, Inc.
PO Box 787
Hudson, OH 44236-0787

ISBN # 1-84360-810-3
ISBN MS Reader (LIT) ISBN # 1-84360-718-2
Other available formats (no ISBNs are assigned):
Adobe (PDF), Rocketbook (RB), Mobipocket (PRC) & HTML

Edited by *Heather Osborn*.
Cover art by *Darrell King*.

FETISH

Sherri L. King

For D.

In memory of Squaker

1992-2003

A friend of a friend, he was more than a friend; he was a perfect kitty cat.

.

Prologue

Aerin looked into the smooth, glassy surface of the pond. She didn't care that the cold, damp of the ground was soaking into the fabric of her serviceable grey skirt. Didn't care that the mud and rocks on the small shoreline of the water's playful edge were scuffing her black leather pumps. Nothing so inconsequential could have mattered to her in that moment. For the first time in weeks she'd caught sight of her reflection...and she was trapped, held riveted by what she saw in the water-mirror.

The face reflected in the depths of the pond was too round, far too plump, and full of too many shameful stresses. The soft, brown hair was straight and unappealing, lying in a bodiless hood over her round skull. Her brown eyes were set too close together, and wrinkled from too much squinting behind her thick-rimmed glasses. Her nose was too large. Her skin far too pale.

Nothing she saw made her the least bit happy to be caught in her own skin.

This was why she never looked into mirrors. Being fat her whole life, being ugly and plain and *boring*, had made her avoid any reflective surfaces like the plague. But she'd never reacted like this, with such self-loathing and pity. Nothing had changed enough for her to recoil so violently to this unexpected glimpse into the pond. Except for one thing.

Somehow, she'd gotten old. On top of everything else, now she was no longer young.

She shuddered, looking at the image of her own hated face. Time had ravaged that face with a brutal, merciless glee. *My god...I'm forty-seven years old. Forty-seven.* Somehow she'd ignored it; until now she'd never bothered to give it much thought. But here the truth of it, at last, struck her like a blow. The salad days of her life were behind her, nothing was left for her now but the routine of tomorrow and tomorrow and hopefully, if she was lucky...another tomorrow.

"I've never done anything spectacular with my life," she whispered into the watery-mirror, suddenly frightened, "I've never been anybody special. Never felt anything," she swallowed hard, "*real.*"

And when had she ever had the chance? A fat, ugly, brainiac nerd like her rarely got any sort of chance for adventure or love or any of what made life worth living. She wasn't stupid; she knew how people saw her. How people always saw her — and all of the others who were unlucky enough to be as physically ill-favored as she.

She was a desk worker. Her world was a relatively safe one, for all of its sometimes cutthroat atmosphere. A world of tight cubicle walls and impersonal colleagues. She was a typesetter at a small printing company, designing and laying out wedding invitations, business cards, letterheads and the like, for thousands of paying customers throughout the region. The job paid well and took no small amount of speed and skill, which was a boost for her ego. But it was also the type of job that required nothing of its workers in the way of personality or looks.

But oh, if she'd been someone else—someone prettier—she'd have done something different with her life. With good looks, she'd have never been so painfully shy, and maybe she would have had the courage to pursue a career as a dancer (which she'd always secretly longed to be), or perhaps an art dealer, or even an entrepreneur. With a svelte body she'd have surely married early in life, instead of reaching the age of forty-seven—*forty-seven*—with her virginity still intact. Or maybe she would have never married at all, but taken many lovers instead, just for the fun and variety of it all.

For the adventure.

She splashed her hand weakly into the pond, breaking its smooth surface into hundreds of ripples that each reflected a perfectly wretched, distorted image of her face. Her *hated* face. She splashed the water again. Fat droplets splattered up as a result, wetting her cheeks so that the water from the pond lingered and mixed with the tears that already drew their tracks down her cheeks. How she hated and loathed her face. Hated and loathed herself. All two hundred plus pounds of herself.

Groaning, she rose clumsily and backed away from the all-too-brutally-honest body of water. The well-kept grounds of the park came back into her consciousness as she tried valiantly to dry her tears and straighten her clothes. Blaming out of control hormones (the dratted change of life was already full upon her and wreaking havoc with her emotions), she strove to overcome the harsh moments before the reflective pool. Hating herself for her weakness, she brushed lingering mud and leaves from her panty hose.

I am no weakling. I am not so self-absorbed that a mere glimpse of my reflection should make me blubber like a baby.

Aerin cleared her throat of the last lingering vestiges of tears. Her thick fingers, trembling, but only slightly, pushed her heavy glasses farther up the bridge of her nose. They had slipped as she bent over the pond, and she hated how they made the tip of her nose itch when they fell low. She hated glasses, period. But her eyes were too damaged for even the most radical laser surgery, and at forty-seven it seemed a little late to even give consideration to contact lenses. She'd been wearing glasses since she was seven years old and would undoubtedly wear them until the day she died.

It was difficult, but she rallied her spirits. It was, after all, Friday. And Friday was her favorite day of the week. The day when she had two whole days of freedom to look forward to. The day when a long, hard week of work was at last behind her. Every week was long and hard. Every weekend was a forty-eight hour period of rest and recuperation, and long hours with books and gardening and quilting. Friday was a boon, her own very favorite day. A transitional day.

Lunch hour was almost over. Aerin's plain, brown-paper-wrapped mayonnaise and lettuce sandwich lay uneaten on the park bench behind her. She had no memory of leaving that bench, only remembered seeing her face so suddenly and starkly before her unprepared eyes. Maybe she'd fallen. Maybe she'd crawled down from that bench, onto the damp ground, towards the water, without even consciously meaning to do it. Compulsive behavior had been second nature for her ever since the first faint signs of menopause had awakened her in the night with feverish hot flashes.

She hoped no one had seen her odd behavior.

Who was she kidding? No one gave her a second glance. More often than not, if they happened to see her, they looked quickly the other way—as if they were ashamed to see such a vision of overweight drudgery. Of course no one had seen her moment of self-pity. They were too busy heaping their pity upon her. No, that was too harsh of her. She was forcing her own low self-opinion onto others, when she had no idea how they really felt about her, when they likely felt or noticed nothing at all.

Aerin hated herself for that, too.

Picking up her sandwich with a disgusted grimace, she started the short walk back to the office. It was a lovely day. Cool and gray—nothing odd there, as this was Seattle and almost every day was like this—but today the song of birds was in the air and the scent of spring was in the breeze. And such a lovely, clean breeze it was.

A piece of paper, blown by that very breeze, flew up and shoaled against her blouse and jacket. It tangled there, trembling for but a second. Long enough for Aerin's clumsy, impatient grab at it. Long enough for her to read the machine-printed words inscribed upon it.

It was an ad for some sort of a nightclub. Nothing unusual. Nothing exciting. But, inexplicably, her heart jumped. Her pulse picked up its pace. And her gaze flew over the text not once, but four times before she could manage to tear her gaze away.

Fetish

*Here every fantasy can be indulged with safety and with care. Be and do everything you've ever imagined. At **Fetish**, nothing is taboo.*

That was it. Only those few words and a local cell-phone number. Fetish. What an interesting and apropos name for a place where 'every fantasy' could be indulged. Her lips twisted. She'd never heard of such a place, of course, because she'd never made a habit of visiting themed nightclubs before. Or any night club for that matter, themed or otherwise.

But...*but.*

Maybe there was a first time for everything. Not ten minutes ago she was bemoaning the long years of her life and the lack of excitement she'd encountered therein. Maybe this was a way she could create some excitement for herself. In a place where, so long as the color of her money was green, it didn't matter who she was, or what she looked like.

It was shameful. It was frightening. But she was forty-seven years old, and so scared of that fact that she'd ignored it until the realization of it bit deep, with enough pain to make her weep. Fright or shame had no place in the thought that maybe, just maybe, Fetish — or another club like it, if this one proved a little too much to take — could be the soothing balm for her unexpected brush with a mid-life crisis.

And after all, it was Friday. The weekend lay before her, along with all its endless possibilities. She clutched the paper in fingers gone suddenly desperate, before firmly tucking the ad into the inner breast pocket of her suit jacket. Her dull, gray, suit jacket.

Aerin winced and hurried back to work as quickly as her thick ankles could comfortably carry her.

Chapter One
Two weeks later

Madame Delilah—obviously a sort-of stage-name—smiled at Aerin across the large, walnut desk. It was not an unkind smile. Aerin was thankful for that. Finding herself seated in a room walled with glinting mirrors, across from a woman who was purported to be the Madame of a very expensive, very elite—if somewhat kinky—sex club, was not a comfortable experience. Aerin knew she needed all the kindness this woman could give her right now, or she feared she might bolt.

"I-I'm not sure I should be here," she heard herself say. Wincing, she wondered if her mouth had a mind all its own. How stupid she must sound. Not at all worldly, and it was obvious the patrons of this club were *very* worldly.

They had to be, to spend five thousand bucks a night for a room here.

Madame Delilah's smile never faltered. If anything, it appeared to deepen at Aerin's obvious discomfort. The woman, much younger than she, reached out and took Aerin's trembling hands in her own.

"And that is why you *do* belong here. What we do within these walls is not only for pleasure, but for personal enrichment. When you leave here tomorrow morning, you'll feel better about yourself and your place in the world. I guarantee it, sweetheart."

Aerin swallowed hard and said what was bothering her most about this transaction. What had bothered her most from the beginning. It shamed her. It was her money after all, and this was business…but there was that niggling feeling of shame and doubt that dogged her heels unmercifully. She had to say what was on her mind, to ease her conscience, if only a little. "But what if I'm so disgusting that no-one wants to do this? What if these men, these…" she faltered.

"Escorts," Madame Delilah offered gently. Aerin had come to believe, after just a small bit of contact with this woman, that she had a good and kind heart, even if she was also an efficient, no-nonsense businesswoman.

"Yes." Aerin let out a long, pent-up breath. She hadn't even realized she'd been holding it. "These escorts. What if they can't bear the sight of me?" She looked into the eyes of the other woman. The attractive, slim, and obviously *shrewd* woman. "How can I take that kind of rejection?" she finished lamely, hating herself for sounding so pitifully spineless.

Madame Delilah squeezed her hands reassuringly. "I won't lie to you Aerin. These men have the right to say no. I'm no pimp. My boss—the owner of this establishment—is no pimp. The men and women who work and live here are not prostitutes. What they do, what they *choose* to do, in the company of our clients is their private business.

"But these people are here for a reason, besides the money involved. These people are here to make someone like you happy. To make themselves happy in the endeavor. And, sweetheart, no matter what you may think, you do have charm, and you do have attraction. And I know someone here will help you to see that truth about yourself. You won't leave here with a feeling of rejection. I can almost swear to that."

Aerin avoided the woman's glinting gaze. "You must think I'm pretty pathetic."

"No I don't." The words sounded sincere. "I think you're the perfect client for Fetish."

"You made it sound like so much more than just any old, mundane club when we spoke on the phone. I...I had to try it." Aerin had no idea why, but she'd just *had* to. Three phone conferences with this woman had convinced her. She'd been compelled to come here. To meet this woman.

To meet the man who might — oh how she hoped he might, whoever he was — introduce her to a long overdue state of womanhood.

But that would be in a later visit, if she felt it was worth the money and pride to repeat this event. *This* visit was to introduce her to Fetish and all it had to offer. It was true; this was no lowly, seedy club as she might have feared in the beginning. This was a...Aerin had no name for it. Retreat, maybe. Burlesque house might be too absurdly stereotypical. After talking to Madame Delilah at length she really didn't know what to call this place. Because she'd never heard of such a wonderland as this.

A haven where whatever you wanted was available. Was acceptable. Was encouraged. Sex was only a part of that package. Aerin hadn't asked, but she assumed legalities held no sway over what a client might want. Fetish was a large mansion; a veritable castle, such as it was, outwardly comprised of huge quantities of gray stone, resting nearly fifty miles outside of Seattle. Situated in a secluded expanse of woodland forest, there was every opportunity for illegal and illicit behavior. Aerin had no doubt about that.

Five thousand dollars a night should buy many comforts, be they legal or otherwise. Aerin could afford it, squirreling spinster that she was. She was paid very well. She was very good at her job and deserved the money she earned. But it was still a lot of money to spend, and on something she wasn't even sure was a wise endeavor. She had no idea what to expect in the next few hours—from sundown to sunrise—and had no idea if she'd even want to come back.

She would have to play it by ear.

Madame Delilah drew her back into the present, into their conversation. "This is anything but a mundane club, Aerin. I hope you'll get rid of any preconceived notions now, before I lead you to the common room where the escorts and clients begin their nights. Things are rarely what they may seem on the surface, not here or anywhere else in the world. That's a fact of life and always has been. But you came here for some fun, and perhaps a little boost to your self-esteem, and that is exactly what you will get. If nothing else, you'll have that at least. Your grand adventure."

Aerin started. That was exactly how she'd been thinking of this, in the depths of her own mind. Her *grand adventure*. The one and only in all her long years. And this woman had known. Aerin looked into the woman's knowing eyes and felt herself sinking, nearly drowning in that glittering gaze.

Shaking her head to clear it of such fanciful—and unsettling—notions, she was relieved when the Madame broke their eye-contact and looked away. "I'm ready to start," she said in a near whisper.

"Remember the rules. Leave at first light, alone. If you decide to come back—and I hope you do—come at dusk, alone. We'll have no drunken revelry unless it's in the comfort and privacy of your room and with willing participants. If anyone should make an unwelcome advance, or inconvenience you in any way, you will report it at once to one of the escorts or chaperones. Do not stray from the areas I show you in our tour, unless accompanied by an escort. And honey," the woman leaned over and took her hands again. Aerin hadn't noticed when her hands had been released the first time, and was further unsettled by this lapse in her awareness. "Have fun. I could sense, even through our phone conversations, that there's too little of that in your life. Feel safe here. Feel comfortable. Be yourself, as you want to be, not as our image-conscious society has forced you to be. You're no different from any other human being. You deserve a little happiness of your own."

"Even if it's paid for?" Aerin tried not to sound bitter.

"Yes." Madame Delilah's kind eyes shifted and twinkled strangely. "Even if it's paid for. Especially if it's paid for." She rose from her seat behind the massive desk. "Come on. It's time for the tour, for you to familiarize yourself with the grounds and perhaps find some company as you do so. You paid handsomely for the experience," there it was, another echo of Aerin's thoughts spoken aloud between them, "and time is money or so I've heard. The evening is starting. Your adventure has begun."

The fine hairs on the back of Aerin's neck prickled and stood on end.

* * * * *

"She's here. I sent her on alone to the sitting room."

"No one will approach her before I get there?"

"Unless you should will it otherwise, she'll be left for you." A pause. "Are you sure this is wise?"

"Your phone conversations piqued my curiosity. She sounded very interesting, as you said she would. Now she's here. And it has been a long time since my last…"

"I know. Too long. We all feel you've been remiss in seeing to your own needs."

"My needs are few, but they are there nonetheless. The pity of it is that I have been too busy for companionship of late. Perhaps tonight, if she is as interesting as she sounded over the phone, I will rectify that."

"I hope so."

"She is in the initiate's sitting room?"

"Yes. You'll know her when you see her, I think. She's even more than I expected, and I expected much."

"Very good. Thank you Delilah."

The Madame smiled, and if the topic of this strange conversation could have seen such a smile, she would have run screaming from the club, never to return. "Have a good evening."

"I'm counting on it."

* * * * *

Aerin brought the glass of champagne to her lips. More out of habit than of thirst, really. The glass was there and so she drank from it. Besides, holding the glass helped give her hands something to do besides violently shake on the ends of heavy, weak arms. And maybe—hopefully—a generous dose of alcohol would help calm her ragged nerves.

She fidgeted in her new clothes, bought especially for the occasion. The short-sleeved, doe-brown, silk blouse fit a little snug over her breasts, but was otherwise loose and therefore tolerable. The black slacks were well tailored and quite feminine. Nonetheless she felt a little awkward in them, as the ankles were boot-cut with a flare that was subtle but still quite dramatic when compared with her usual attire. Her shoes were new as well, cute little Italian style half-boots with a heel, though she vaguely wondered if someone of her stature shouldn't avoid such dainty fashions.

Aerin often chose drab styles to downplay her size— though had she but known it, the spinsterish look merely accentuated her breasts and hips in a way she would have abhorred. She'd always promised herself that one day she would break free of her misgivings and dress as wildly as her tastes sometimes ran—perhaps she'd even dare to wear a velvet dress—but she'd never found the courage to do so. She'd made an unusual attempt tonight and had turned herself out quite nicely.

If only she could stop fidgeting.

This was turning out to be a lot more difficult than she'd expected. And she'd expected quite a bit of difficulty. For the millionth time she chided herself for being so stupid as to get suckered into this little pleasure-club thing. It wasn't at all what she'd expected—but then, if asked, she couldn't have said exactly *what* she'd been expecting in the first place — and so far she didn't see how it could be worth her five grand.

Oh, there was plenty of luxury here. The owner of the establishment spared no expense to see to his visitors' comforts. The furnishings alone must have set him back several hundred thousand dollars. The pricey Cristal champagne was flowing freely, along with the caviar and Foie Gras. And the people milling about looked as though they were accustomed to such luxuries, as if they expected them.

No amount of champagne would help her fit in here. No amount of alcohol, hard or soft, would make her more attractive to the escorts here. *God. How could I be so stupid? Why did I even think of coming here, let alone go through with it? I must have been insane.*

No. Just desperate. Completely and utterly, heart-wrenchingly desperate.

She felt the sting of traitorous tears at the edge of her vision and blinked desperately to combat their spill. Hormones again. Menopausal demons come to say their mischievous hello. That must be it. With a sigh she downed the last of the delicious champagne and set the empty flute down on the nearest waiting tray. She was ready to leave. That glass of over-priced champagne was all she'd get out of this horribly foolish endeavor, and she berated herself for the waste.

Beaten down lower than she'd ever been beaten in her life, she turned and made her way out of the exquisite sitting room, heading towards what she hoped was the front door. It was time for a graceful, if hasty, retreat.

"Mistress, where do you go in such a hurry?" A velvet voice eased the rough edges of what would have soon been outright panic. A large, cool hand fell upon hers, grasping it. Trapping her.

Aerin felt both cold and hot at the same time. Fear and relief melded until she wanted to sob. Someone had reached out. Someone had noticed her.

It wasn't all that she'd hoped for, but it was a start. It was a balm to her wounded heart. She wouldn't have to leave this place in total defeat. At least she'd exchange a sentence or two with someone who wasn't in charge of billing her credit card upon entrance.

Turning her head towards the voice was easy. Meeting the face of the stranger who owned it was more difficult. What she saw shocked her through and through, down to her marrow.

Of all the things she'd expected, she hadn't expected this—this *kindness*—from such a handsome, appealing man.

How tall he was! It was the first thing she noticed, but not the last. He was well over six feet. Perhaps half a foot over that. Where most men who attained that height would have been thin or lanky, this man was powerful and well muscled. His shoulders were so broad they filled her vision. Dressed as he was in a plain black t-shirt and bondage pants—the well-fitting kind with shiny silver buckles and loops—every delineated muscle was accentuated to perfection.

His neck was thick and corded, though just shy of looking brutish. His arms seemed long, longer than his frame—large as it was—should have required. His torso, too, was long. It tapered almost dramatically into a small waist and straight hips. His legs went on for miles and sported thick muscles of their own. A dancer's muscles, maybe. An erotic dancer's muscles, more like.

She trembled.

"Are you alright, Mistress?" he asked gently. His husky, bedroom voice with its decidedly exotic lilt — where could he be from, he certainly wasn't from America? — softened intimately. "Do you need to sit down for a moment? It is perhaps a bit too warm in here?"

Aerin sucked a deep breath into her lungs, realizing with some surprise that they'd been starving for it. She'd been holding her breath the whole time. And how much time had passed, time which she'd spent foolishly ogling him?

Embarrassment stained her cheeks in a flood, warming them fever hot.

The hand that held hers pulled her close as he led her to the nearest divan. The deep, soft brocade of the upholstery was cool against her clothed legs and soothing. The man followed her down upon it, lounging comfortably back farther than she so that his body seemed to cradle hers, gently rubbing his hand up and down her arm as he did so, as if to soothe her. It didn't soothe her at all; in fact, it succeeded in just the opposite.

"May I ask your name, Mistress?" he questioned in a soft, coaxing tone.

"Aerin," she gave it to him freely. The Mistress thing was getting weird, though she knew the 'escorts' were apt to use it, or Master, depending on the sex of the client. She didn't like being Mistress of anything, let alone another person. It was her belief that no amount of money should give her that right.

Besides, it seemed a little sophomoric. And unnecessary. Though he kept calling her Mistress, he in no way sounded deferential or submissive. He sounded as though the word was merely a formality, one ingrained, but not one he infused with any real weight or station. What was the point of titles if they had no real meaning behind them?

"Mistress Aerin," he rolled the word around in his mouth like sweet, decadent candy. There was the 'Mistress' again, and there was no way this man used it in any way other than he might use a Ms. or Mrs. — he didn't seem the type to be subservient to anyone, job requirements or no.

Aerin shook her head slightly. She wasn't one to study people like this and judge them out of hand. The man had spoken a few words to her, that was all. And here she was trying to analyze and label his personality. It was unforgivable. And more than a little pointless. There wasn't much she could learn about a person's true personality under these circumstances anyway. This was business more than anything.

She was paying for this man's kindness. She would do well to remember that. Her warm blush subsided, replaced by a cold feeling of loneliness.

"What has you looking so forlorn, Mistress Aerin? What made you seek an exit so early on such a fine evening as this?"

"Don't call me that."

"Aerin isn't your name?" he asked with a tiny smile and the quirk of a brow.

Aerin pursed her lips. He knew damn well what she meant, and it irked her for some unexplained reason that he should pretend otherwise. "Don't call me Mistress."

"You would prefer Master?" Now he was openly teasing her.

"I just don't like it, okay? Please don't use it."

"May I call you Aerin, then?"

"You know that's what I'd prefer."

His eyes glittered strangely. Dangerously. All his playful teasing vanished, as if it had never been. He rose up higher on the elbow that supported his lazy sprawl, coming close enough that his breath warmed the fine hairs on her arm. "I don't know yet what you'd prefer. But I'd like to learn. I'd very much like to learn all your preferences."

The tears burned her eyes once more, but this time for a different reason. Guilt. Shameful guilt. "You don't have to say that. I don't want you to say that…"

"You don't want my interest in you?" That silky, lilting voice became a physical caress; it ran down her spine like a finger, touched her breasts like lips. Made her wet between her legs.

How did he do that?

Shaking the seduction of his wicked words away, she straightened defensively. "I made a mistake in coming here," and she knew this was the truth. She made as if to rise.

The tips of two fingers settled firmly on the inside of her wrist, upon the desperate beat of her pulse. Somehow, this infinitesimal gesture kept her held captive there with him. "You made no mistake," he breathed, but firmly.

"I don't know why I came," so shaky those words. Her lips trembled with them.

"I know why you came. I know why you'll come again." Arrogant is what he seemed to her now, above all things.

She was analyzing him again. Her mind was in two places at once, one part of it watching — disentangled from the rest of her — while the other part swam drunkenly in the cloying appeal of the man beside her. She didn't like this heretofore undiscovered duality in herself.

"I'm leaving. And I won't come again," she murmured, sounding less firm than she would have liked.

"Don't leave, Aerin." At last, he used her name as she wanted — and it sounded downright wicked on his lips.

"You don't have to convince me to stay. I'm not going to ask for a refund, so don't bother worrying over it."

"Do you think I'm worrying over it?"

Her eyes rose to meet his. They were at once green and silver and blue. Hypnotic. She'd never seen eyes like his. Not even close.

"I don't know," she said. She was confused. What were they talking about?

"Forget why or how you are here, only that you are. That you and I are here, together, is all that matters. Stay with me. Let me show you about the place," he coaxed.

For some reason, she couldn't look away from him. She didn't want to. Not even to preserve her own dignity. Swallowing, she found her tongue, though it was an arduous struggle. "Madame Delilah showed me around already," she lied, inexplicably frightened into a brief moment of self-preservation.

She felt the cool silk of his mouth at her neck before she saw him move. Something was wrong with her eyes. The Cristal, probably. She'd drunk it too quickly. Or maybe her spectacles were crooked, causing her vision to swim and grow dizzy. It could be anything…and it didn't matter, she realized. His mouth was so firm and so soft.

Each word he spoke was a kiss against her skin, soft and devastating. "I can show you more than she. Far more."

Her heart thundered. The sands of a thousand deserts dried her mouth to cracking. Vision swimming, she felt, with the last of her senses, the brush of his fingertip against the swell of her breast. Accepting his will as her own, she gave up the last of her resistance.

And this was how she met Violanti D'Arco.

Chapter Two

"This is the first step of your journey." Violanti—how did she know his name? Had she asked? She couldn't remember now—gestured her forward towards a jade-green door.

"Your name is Violanti?" she asked stupidly.

A small, amused smile appeared upon the lush moue of his mouth. "Yes, and it sounds lovely on your lips."

"It sounds…is it Italian?" She frowned, puzzled that it should matter or that she was even remarking upon it.

The smile disappeared. His eyes glittered from green to silver to blue, making her dizzy. "It is," was his short answer.

"Oh." Forgetting almost instantly what they'd been discussing, she looked beyond him to the green door. "What's in there?" Curiosity like she'd never experienced before nearly overcame her shyness.

That smile of his again. Was it a practiced thing? It was so sensual that it should have been. No man should have such an alluring attribute, without having to work for it a little. "Follow me to find out." He opened the door and stepped inside. Aerin couldn't have stayed behind had she wanted to. And she halfway did. Whatever was waiting behind that door, it made her nervous.

Once she stepped over the threshold, Violanti closed the door softly behind her. Trapping her. Trapping them. Together.

The room was lovely. Not at all sinister or threatening, as she'd feared. Soft hues of jade, accentuated by warm and creamy vanilla, gave the room a soothing and inviting quality. The lush scents of vanilla and perhaps a little apple or pineapple, were thick in the room and flattering to the décor. It added to the comfort of the space.

The perfume lulled Aerin, enveloping her, beckoning and seductive. Violanti's hand at her back coaxed and eased her. She moved further into the room. There was another divan here, piled deep with silk, and emerald in hue. It was positioned before a wall, the only item of furniture in the room that was free of the jade and vanilla motif. Violanti led her to it gently, but firmly, and joined her there upon it.

A light came on somewhere behind the wall they faced, making it transparent. Aerin realized it was a two-way mirror. Behind it, lay another room identical to theirs. Only there were several people in it.

Aerin blushed furiously and looked away. The long, cool fingers of her escort grasped her chin and turned her face back to the scene before them. "Look at them, Aerin. There is no shame in it."

She couldn't help it. She had to look. The blush deepened, burning her neck and breasts hotly. "Do they know we can see them?" Was that her voice, breathless and faint?

He chuckled softly. It was like a whisper, that small laugh. But she felt it vibrate along her very bones. "Of course. It's what they want. It's why they chose that room. They are exhibitionists; it is their fetish to be watched by others, and the club provides this experience for them."

"Can they see us?"

"No. Do you want them to?"

"No!" she exploded. Then, more calmly, "No. I'd rather they didn't. I—I doubt I have an exhibitionistic fetish myself."

Again that amused smile. Amusement at her expense. For a second she both hated and feared that smile and all the mysteries that lay behind it. But the moment came and went, and she went straight back to being dazzled by him, and by the scene unfolding behind the mirror. "I question whether you know your own fetishes, Mistress."

"I told you not to call me that. It makes me uncomfortable."

"Even after being in your own skin the whole of your life, I can see you are uncomfortable there. Why should this be any different that you must take exception?"

She pulled back with a shallow, unsteady breath; surprised that he could both injure and anger her so completely and so swiftly. "You don't know me. You shouldn't make assumptions about people you don't know."

His eyes glittered dangerously. "You made the assumption that I was interested in you out of pity or obligation simply because you paid for your stay here, didn't you?"

She had. Of course she had. It was a safe assumption to make. More than safe.

He seemed to see her admission of it, perhaps in the look of her eyes or face. This Violanti was very observant. "So you are as guilty as I of assumption. And perhaps we are both wrong...no. That's not true. I say you are wrong about me. While I know I'm right about you." He spoke the last with an underlying tone that practically dared her to disagree.

Aerin couldn't disagree, nor could she pretend to. He was right. She was a stranger in her own skin, had always been, and it would ever be so. But that didn't mean she had to approve of his observation of the fact.

"I don't want to talk about this." She glanced at the mirror, what lay beyond it, then looked away. "I shouldn't have come here. I need to go now."

Again, he laid his fingers—the tips of two, no more—against the pulse that beat in her wrist. Had he made any more of a movement, she would have perhaps unearthed the strength to bolt. But, as before, his small gesture effectively stilled her.

"Back to that again? I'm sorry, Aerin. I was being uncouth, forgive me. But I can plainly see that, of all our patrons, you need Fetish desperately. You need the comfort and pleasure we can give. And we can help you to find that hidden self you've so long forgotten. The part of you that isn't afraid of your own sensuality. Of your own sexual appeal. You've buried it deep, but still it is there, waiting for discovery. Let us help you find it. Let *me* help you find it."

"Are you making fun of me?" she asked, shaken.

"No. Never think that. With you I shall always be honest. I promise that to you here and now. Believe it," he smiled that slow honeyed smile, "for I never renege on a promise."

"I don't know what I expected when I came here. And I felt guilty for it as soon as I wrote out the check. I just wanted…" she faltered.

"You wanted love. To be loved, if but for a moment, even if you had to purchase that moment."

"Yes. I'm pathetic."

"No!" His hand was a vice now around her wrist. "Never, ever say such again in my presence. It isn't true. You are precious and lovely and you deserve love, as do all creatures on this Earth. But you have forgotten your due, because society, popular fashion, and marketing have told you to. Aerin, listen to me now as you have never listened to another; you are beautiful."

She shied away, in discomfort and disbelief.

The long fingers of his sculpted hand pulled her chin around to face him, trapping her. "You *are* beautiful, Aerin," he repeated firmly. "Let me show you just how beautiful you are. Let me teach this to you, if nothing else, though you have much to learn."

His eyes were hypnotic, beautiful. She felt like a deer caught in the hunter's floodlights. "I don't want you to be a-a-a whore for m-me," she stuttered.

He laughed down into her face, before ducking his blue-black head to nuzzle his cool, soft lips into the curve of her neck. Chills raced like horses up and down her flesh where he touched her. "I am not a whore, no more than you are."

"But I paid for—"

"Shh." The pad of his thumb traced the fullness of her lower lip, causing it to swell and tingle, engorged with blood and arousal. His hand moved and tangled in the hair at her nape, holding her close, as his lips nuzzled her deep.

"Speak of that no more. What you paid for was a room here in this place, for pleasure and succor if you could find it here; not the soul of any man or woman in these walls. None of us here are obligated in any way to do more than offer drinks or conversation to our patrons. I am here with you now because I choose to be. If we make the beast with two backs — and I'll admit, even this soon, that I long for that with you — then it will be because we both choose to make it." He moved her hand with his, lips still tickling against the pulse of her neck as he did so, and lowered it onto the hard swell at his crotch.

She gasped and tried to pull away. He held her firm and spoke again, each word seeming to be a magical, invisible finger caressing her breasts and mons. "This is my honesty. This is my truth. I desire you. Because you are beautiful. Because you are..." his teeth scraped over her pulse and she moaned, "sweet and innocent and worthy. I desire you."

He let her hand go, and though she was shy, she could not immediately pull away from his erection. This was the first time in her life that she had felt such a thing. It was alien and scary but it was also devastatingly arousing.

He pressed another kiss to her throat, hard, then pulled away. Reaching down he joined their hands, giving hers a reassuring squeeze. He straightened, his broad shoulders actually dwarfing her — for the first time in her life she felt small — and he looked back to the mirror before them. She had almost forgotten it these past few moments.

"Tonight's lesson will be this; watching, *seeing*, can bring pleasure. And there is no shame in that. None. See here, that everyone is the same in their passion. We are all equal. We are all worthy. You are no different in your worth, no matter what you might think to the contrary. So watch with me now, and learn."

Her eyes, burning now, rose to watch the scene unfold behind the mirror.

Five people occupied the room. Three women, two men, all contrasting in color, shape and form. The women were curvaceous and lush, a redhead, a brunette, and a blonde. The men were as night and day, one a brunette with tightly muscled ivory skin and the other a bleached blonde, stoutly built, with a deep, creamy chocolate complexion.

All of them were completely nude, though a few minutes before they had been in various states of undress. They were clearly enjoying themselves; uncaring, or more likely aroused, knowing that someone was watching their play. They certainly showed no shame or awkwardness in the knowledge.

The brunette woman's perfectly round breasts pillowed the head of the man with pale vanilla skin. She lounged, spread-legged, behind and beneath him upon a large four-poster bed. His body was cradled in the spoon of hers. The brunette's long, well-manicured fingers played idly with his hair as she watched the motions of the redheaded woman next to them.

The redhead, pouting lips full and moist with excitement, crouched next to the two, and lifted her large-nippled breasts while leaning into the brunette man seductively; offering him her forbidden fruit. The man's lips closed eagerly about first one nipple, then the other as though suckling a ripe and delicious berry.

The blonde woman—blessed with an hourglass figure that even Marilyn Monroe would have envied—was taking the brunette man's hard, straining dick into her mouth. The red and swollen flesh of his member disappeared and reappeared, over and over, as her head bobbed up and down with her ablutions. His cock was neither small nor large, and not as handsome as some of the cocks Aerin had seen in pornographic films, but the woman deep-throating him clearly didn't care. She smiled happily up at the man each time the mushroom-shaped head of his prick slipped free from her glistening lips.

The gorgeously built, mocha-skinned man watched from the sidelines, sometimes fondling the women, sometimes fondling the man, as he ham-fisted his own swollen organ. His cock was the smaller of the two in the room, but it was quite a bit more attractive than the other man's. It took a moment for Aerin to realize it was mostly because he was shaved completely bald. His balls were tight against his body, two dark, satin-covered stones glistening like warm creamy cocoa in the soft light of the room.

Aerin felt her pussy grow wet. Wetter.

Because the participants of the small orgy were nude, Aerin wasn't sure who worked at Fetish and who didn't. The club escorts all wore black, from neck to toe, so they were relatively easy to spot in the common rooms. But here, as Violanti had mentioned earlier, these people seemed equal. Here in the room of lust and desire, there were no escorts, no patrons, only lovers. For some reason this soothed Aerin's niggling sense of guilt, and she was grateful at least for that.

The brunette man lying on the bed suddenly pushed his mouthful of breast away and motioned his chocolate-skinned lover closer. The dark god of a man stopped fondling himself and climbed upon the bed, straddled the brunette man's chest, and slipped the length of his gorgeous black cock into his partner's mouth. Aerin gasped in surprise, but could not look away from the decadent sight.

The brunette on the bed suckled that beautiful dark cock and squeezed his hands tight around the man's buttocks, pulling him even more intimately close. The blonde Marilyn performing fellatio upon the lounging man stopped and allowed the redhead to climb upon the man's wetly shining penis.

The redhead wrapped her arms around the waist of the ebony man in front of her as she impaled herself on his partner and together they undulated upon their lounging lover. They looked so exotic, she with her pale skin, he with his creamy blackness, wrapped together almost lovingly as they moved in rhythm.

'Marilyn' came around and kissed the lounging brunette woman whose breasts still pillowed the now ecstatically groaning man. The two women fondled each other's breasts, tongues licking at each other's mouths, hungrily. Their hair mixed in shades that echoed the skin tones of their lovers.

Together, the group was a mass of writhing, sweating bodies awash in an ever-shifting, titillating kaleidoscope of color.

Aerin felt hot. Her heart thundered. She'd never expected she might spend the night in this fashion, watching the most erotic peep show imaginable.

"Do you like watching them, Aerin?"

She couldn't speak. Could barely breathe. She nodded instead, not thinking to lie or be embarrassed in such a nakedly erotic moment, knowing that she did indeed like watching them. She liked it very much.

"Good. I felt certain you would. Now for the next step on your journey."

Chapter Three

Aerin started in surprise.

Violanti's eyes were hot as molten steel...completely silver now. Glittering and bright in the soft light of the room. He rose from his seat beside her, and moved behind the chaise where she could no longer see him. Aerin was too nervous to watch, to turn and openly study his movements, so she was surprised that he had found another soft, cushioned chair, which he now moved to set directly in front of her. He sat upon it, long legs reaching out until they tangled with hers.

"Are you ready?"

Aerin swallowed, mouth gone dry as a desert in a long drought. "R-ready for what?"

"I told you that this night's lesson would teach you to watch and enjoy what you see. You have said you enjoyed watching the lovers in the mirror and that is good. Now, you must discover the very real difference between having the barrier of that window between you and what you see versus not having it there at all."

"I don't think —"

He leaned forward, bringing their faces close, so close that she could almost taste the sweet sugar of his breath on her mouth. "You don't have to think. You've only to *see*, to watch."

He leaned back once more and sighed softly. That long breath was incredibly titillating, reaching down to echo in Aerin's womb. His hands moved, slowly caressing himself, moving down his well-muscled chest, to his flat abdomen, then at long last to the button of his pants.

It was then that Aerin fully realized what he intended. The blush in her cheeks intensified until she thought her skin would burst into flames, but no force on Earth could have made her look away from those long fingers of his as they opened the button and fly.

"The mirror protects you, Aerin. From yourself more than from the lovers. With the mirror for a barrier, you don't feel a need to guard your reaction or arousal. But without that mirror, you would feel naked, exposed. You would not let yourself get lost in the show."

He was right. Aerin trembled.

His pants were undone. With one hand he pulled his shirt up high upon his belly, revealing a smooth expanse of rigid, muscled flesh. The other hand slowly delved into the open fabric at his crotch.

"I will show you that you needn't ever hide your reaction, your arousal, your enjoyment, be there a mirror or no. Never hide behind a wall, Aerin, real or metaphorical. There is no joy in hiding. Be open to the world. Be open to your lovers. There is no greater eroticism than the show of honest emotion."

His hand cupped the bulge of his arousal and lifted. Aerin's breath caught. The pants gaped wide and the full length of his cock was revealed to her starving gaze. It was dusky, smooth, and long. So thick and wide Aerin knew she'd never be able to wrap her hand around it if she were to try.

A tracery of blue veins decorated it, thin and delicate, there just beneath the velvet skin. It looked heavy and hard, curving slightly to the right upon his stomach beneath the hand he still held cupped around its base. The crown was large, but not so large that it was fatter than the thickest part of him. It had a swooping, round ridge that led up to the hole upon the very crest.

A small drop of clear, glistening liquid wept from the hole and slowly trailed down over the fat head.

Aerin's eyes followed it, hypnotized.

"Watch me, Aerin. Be not shy. Never that, not with me. As you watch me, I will watch you. Show me your desire. Show me your need and I will show you mine."

Aerin watched, riveted, as his hand cupped that heavy flesh more firmly, as it began to move up and down in a pistoning motion. The crown wept its glistening tears and his hands captured them, swirled them upon the shaft, using it for lubrication.

"Do you like what you see, Lady?" His voice was a hoarse, soft whisper.

"Yes," she answered him in kind, and it was the truth, but so much more than that. She was enthralled, her body a humming throb of sharp arousal that offered no surcease. The wicked knife's edge of that arousal cut her deep and made her body ache with unrequited longing. Her thighs trembled and her weeping pussy juices soaked through the cloth of her panties.

His eyes were hooded now, showing the barest slit of color, glittering once more with those ever changing hues. His lashes were long, spiky, and black as the darkest, moonless night. They veiled his eyes and brushed his high cheekbones, teasing Aerin, affording her only brief glimpses of the fire of his gaze.

"Will you touch yourself, as I do?" he asked huskily.

"I can't," she moaned. Her lips were dry and she licked them. Violanti's eyes saw it all and burned ever more brightly.

His lashes rose, his gaze was piercing, demanding. "You can."

"No. You can't ask me to—"

"Then I am no longer asking. I am telling you. Touch yourself as I do. Feel no shame in it, Aerin, feel no shyness. I want to see you. I *need* to see you."

At last she found the strength to look away. But there was no safety in that gesture, for behind him was the scene of the lovers, still at play, in the world beyond the mirror. "I can't. I won't. It's too soon." She hated herself for her cowardice, but it wouldn't change the fact that she simply *couldn't* fondle herself openly before this man.

A puff of impatient breath exploded from his tight lips. "Very well then. I'll not push you. Tonight. But there will come a time, soon, when you will do as I bid. As I beg. As I demand. Now. Watch. And learn that there is no shame in wanting, in need, or in sharing either of those things."

He leaned his head back upon the chair. The line of his chin and throat was an expanse of beautiful, corded muscle in a smooth sheath of bronze skin. That skin glistened in the soft light of the room, so different from the flesh of any man Aerin had ever seen. It had a hypnotic lure all its own, she could hardly think to look away from it, from that column of throat and neck which sloped into broad shoulders.

She both hoped and feared that he might remove his shirt. That all that naked skin, revealed at once, would be a sight to devil her dreams for the rest of her life. It would be such sinful decadence, the sight of him nude. And oh how she wanted that.

Skin and sin—such meaningful words, both imbued with the power to drive a woman mad with lust.

At last she managed to look down, down, past the strong throat, past the broad shoulders, down the long torso...to the place she was most eager to see.

That beautiful weapon—that gorgeous cock—disappeared and reappeared inside his stroking fist. Over and over in that wondrous rhythm. Pump, pump, pump. Thrust, thrust, thrust. Aerin's heart was soon echoing this rhythm, playing its own sweet song of arousal.

His hips bucked. Once. Twice. His cock was swollen ever larger, ever harder, the head blushed a dark, dark rouge. Like lipstick. Aerin wanted to kiss it. Her mouth actually hurt with the intensity of that desire. She licked her lips.

"That will come later, Aerin," he seemed to read her mind. "For now, just watch."

She did. In the back of her mind, she realized their breaths had synchronized. Their breathing escalated with the faster motions of his hand and his hips. His testicles were hard, drawn tight beneath his wide cock. The large round weight of them were suddenly straining for the ultimate release, with an impatience that was readily apparent in the quickening pace of Violanti's fists.

It seemed he gripped himself even tighter. Aerin saw his jaw bulge as he gritted his teeth. His eyelashes were fluttering, his eyes gazing into hers one moment, and then rolling wildly the next, like some maddened animal. His back bowed in the chair, his hips bucked and undulated. He was close...so very close to the edge of his climax.

Aerin felt that edge as if she, too, were joining him there. Tiny pulsing heartbeats washed through her breasts and mons. Her clit was a swollen throb at the apex of her pussy, which was so flooded with moisture it should have shocked her. Aerin had never been so wet, so aroused. Not ever, not like this. And without even touching herself…it was incredible.

"Watch me, Aerin," he moaned in a straining whisper. "Look and see me, Lady, see me come for your pleasure."

How could she have looked away in such a powerful moment? There was no force in heaven or hell that could have pulled her gaze away as he thrust mightily upwards in his chair. His cock bobbed as his hand moved lightning quick up and down the length. His balls trembled. And then he came.

With a deep, tortured groan wrenched up from the depths of him, Violanti's eyes squeezed shut. His lips pursed tightly, then moued around another groan. His body shuddered and his cock swelled. Pulsed. His hand paused, gripping tightly. A thick, creamy white eruption of fluid spurted up over his fist and onto his stomach.

Aerin moaned. He groaned its echo and another eruption spilled free from his swollen cock.

His hand started moving again, his hips bucking against the uncontrollable force that milked him of his ecstasy. His pants had fallen to his knees with his movements, and so he spread his legs wider, bucked harder into his hand. Aerin saw the dark shadows that led beneath his sac as he moved. Her eyes burned. So did her pussy.

She would have given anything in that moment for the courage to climb atop his heaving body. But she couldn't even find enough courage to touch herself before him, let alone ride him. This failing tore at her heart, but did nothing to free her from the longing — the fever — that gripped her.

Another spurt of come flew onto his stomach, and then he subsided. His hand still moved, but more slowly now upon that red and glistening shaft. The scent of him — cinnamon and almond and musky man — assailed her, drowned her. She wondered if he would taste as good as he smelled and grew pleasantly dizzy with the thought.

Her eyes followed his other hand as it rose and rubbed that wonderful cream onto his stomach and up higher, pushing the shirt out of the way as he did. His olive-toned, hairless chest peeked out at her and she moaned again. Small amounts of glistening semen still wept from his cock as he continued to gently stroke himself, but he didn't seem to mind. He was covered with the shine of his sex from chest to cock and appeared to enjoy it completely.

Aerin wanted to touch him, wanted to feel that most private essence of him.

His fingers dipped into the last remaining droplets upon the head of his cock, and brought them up to his mouth. He licked his fingers clean, with slow laps of his tongue. His eyes opened once more and locked with hers, trapping her.

"Next time you'll join me, won't you Aerin?"

She trembled and could not find her voice to answer. Indeed, she had no idea what she would have said could she have answered.

Violanti was suddenly crouched before her, parting her legs with strong and purposeful hands. His pants were still at his knees and the long column of his cock brushed against her like a firebrand. The scent of his sex inebriated her, seduced her, beckoned her. A perfumed cloud of his delicious male musk. Her mouth watered.

His mouth lowered.

"N-no, what are you doing?" she flustered, finding her voice at last, pushing at his hands.

"I cannot resist the lure of the passion — the longing — I see in your eyes." Ignoring her protests, his hands moved, stroking the insides of her thighs softly, tantalizing her to madness.

"No. Don't." She spoke that last more firmly than she would have thought possible. "Please don't."

"I can smell that you want me. I can almost taste it on the air between us. Do you deny that you want me?"

"No. I do want you." Gads, what warm-blooded woman wouldn't after such an intimate show? "But *please*, I can't do this."

His eyes burned into hers. Was there anger there in their multi-colored depths? They were at first hard, then soft, then hard again. As if he warred with himself. "You can do this," he gritted out, voice rough like a growl.

"I-I..." She didn't know what she wanted. Her eyes darted back up toward the mirror behind him, but again there was no safety in looking there. Her body rained down its never-ending arousal like a flood of fire between her legs as she watched the climax of the blond man stream like milk into the mouth and face of the brunette man.

She'd never seen so much semen, and never in person, only in pornographic movies — movies she'd used to find her own arousal as she'd brought herself to completion over the years. In no way had they prepared her for the explosive rush of seeing such release firsthand.

Violanti commanded her attention once more. "Let me have this from you. Your passion. Your desire. Your arousal. I need them, as much or more than even you do."

"I don't want this, not this way. You don't really want it either, you—"

"Don't tell me what I want!" his voice thundered, and Aerin wondered that the people behind the mirror couldn't hear it.

Violanti's eyes were at once that odd shifting color of green and silver and blue, though the shifts were much quicker now than ever they had been. Aerin wondered how such eyes could exist in nature, but she'd certainly never heard of contacts that could change color. Perhaps his eyes were some sort of weird hazel she'd never seen, that they changed so from one hue to the next.

Calmer now, quieter, he continued. "Don't tell me what I want, never think you have that power. Let me, instead, tell you. Let me tell you all that I desire."

Her heart shuddered, her breath stalled. His hands strayed higher, and the tips of his fingers fluttered against her sex.

"I desire to lay you back on this couch and end all your misgivings about yourself, about your body, and especially about me. I want to spread your legs wide and lay my tongue against the wet heart of you. I want to pillow my head against your breasts, taste the berries of your nipples, and have your nails rake lines into my back while I do so. I desire to slip my cock into your wet cunt and ride you until you bruise, with your ankles about my neck and my fingers digging into your sweetly cushioned bottom. That's what I desire. That's what I want. And none of your misgivings about Fetish or about your place in it will change that."

One of his hands cupped her fully and, reflexively more than defensively, she clenched her legs tightly shut around it. "H-how can you want that?" She nearly moaned the words. "Just look at me! You can't want that." Her hands flew to her face, hiding herself even as she commanded he see her for what she was. An overweight, middle-aged spinster. Surely no man as beautiful or as sensual as he could find an attraction to such a pitiful thing.

Violanti disentangled himself from her legs and used both hands to lower hers from her face. They were smooth and damp from his release and she moaned softly at their touch. "You are beautiful, Aerin. You are. But if you're not ready to see that yet, then perhaps I can wait. But I cannot wait for long. Don't ask that of me. Don't ask that of yourself. We both deserve your passion. We both deserve your pleasure. We both hunger for it, as though we starved."

The taste of tears filled her mouth and she realized with some surprise that she was weeping. Apologetic, she found the strength to meet his gaze with her own. "I thought I could do this. I thought I could go through with it."

His smile was bitter, twisted somehow. "No you didn't. You thought you would meet with disappointment, with rejection, and validate your own low sense of self-worth. You didn't expect to be given a different view, not on anything."

Defensive now, she pursed her lips. "No. I paid for sex, didn't I? I certainly don't need to pay five grand to feel sorry for myself."

"You didn't pay for sex. You paid for pleasure. And I think, deep down, you believe that the only pleasure you can find is in the rejection and dismissal of others. That's what you paid for…but you're getting something else for your money, and I don't think you were at all prepared for it."

"We're back to assumptions now. I thought we were done with that," she bit out, angry with him for his ability to see her. Really *see* her…and was she truly like that? It scared her to realize that she just might be.

"Assumption has nothing to do with it. One day you'll see that I have my own ways of knowing you, to the depths of your soul. It's why I'm here at Fetish. This is my gift, my value to others. In the end you'll see it as a value yourself."

"But I won't come back here to find that out. I'm not coming back here, so stop saying all that. I don't need a shrink, Violanti. In any case, a shrink would probably be cheaper, so don't try to analyze me. I doubt you'll get a chance to convince me of anything in the few hours left of the night, so please just quit with the whole Don Juan act. There's no reason for it."

He fingered a lock of her hair, eyes hooded. "I'm sorry the world has given you such a hard and bitter shell to crouch inside of. I'm sorry that you're not happy. I'm sorry that you're lonely. But won't you let that go for one night? One night with me?"

The soft velvet timbre of his voice was devastating her senses. She so desperately wanted to lie back and let him do all those things he said he wanted to do. But something held her back, something deep inside of her. Perhaps it was fear, perhaps it was something else, something indefinable even in her deepest heart. Only one certainty gripped her, she couldn't be with him, knowing it was possibly the color of her money that had sparked his interest.

As a virgin, as a woman, as *Aerin Peters*, she couldn't bring herself to take this man as a lover under such conditions.

"Not tonight," she heard herself say. "Tonight, let's just talk okay? You said I paid for pleasure and I did. But I think most of all, the pleasure I want tonight is that of your company. Of your voice and words. That's all." Her eyes met his, and she knew the plea that swam behind her lashes was plain for him to see. The plea for understanding. For reprieve. "Be my friend tonight Violanti, not my paid escort."

The smile he gave her was perhaps the most genuine yet, though it seemed tinged with some small regret. "Very well then. Perhaps later you'll be ready for more. But for tonight, we will be as friends, because you will it so."

With a sigh, Aerin wondered if she'd blown her one chance at taking a lover. Then forgot about it, as Violanti motioned for her to continue watching the mirror. The rest of the night passed in a pleasant blur. Her body tingled with the sensuality of the view and of her company. Her mind buzzed with the pleasure of friendly conversation. Her heart and soul smiled with happiness and content and it was good.

The night was over so quickly, Aerin didn't even go to her room to sleep. She spent the whole of it with him. The hour of dawn came all too soon, the time for goodbye and farewell. Violanti kissed her on both cheeks, squeezing her hands before he left to find his own room in the bowels of the club. Aerin watched him go with an unexpected pain in her heart.

Aerin drove her Honda home with a feeling of joy and regret. As midday came she was confused by the realization that there was no clear memory of Violanti's face or even what they had talked about during the evening hours. Then came the realization that perhaps she didn't have to remember any of it. Particulars didn't matter. It was the lingering happiness that would supply her with all the memories she would need in the bleak days to come as her life resumed its normal routine.

She only wished she could remember his face.

* * * * *

"How was she?"

"All I had hoped for and more. I think she will come back. Sooner rather than later, I should wager."

"But you still seem too pale. Drawn. Tired." Violanti's face tightened, closed out any sign of emotion, and Delilah immediately regretted her assessing words. "Forgive me — "

"No. There is nothing to forgive. I am all that you say."

"Perhaps tomorrow night — "

"We only open our doors once a week. No exceptions."

"But, with *you*, one of the men would gladly share — "

"There is no need for that. I will wait for her to come around again. Next week I should think. I don't believe that's too much to wish for."

"You work too hard," Delilah sighed, knowing it was no use continuing the conversation. Violanti was the most stubborn man she'd ever encountered—and she'd encountered a great many throughout the course of her life.

His face softened, looking almost wistful in the dim light of the passageway that led to their living quarters. "She fairly glowed."

"She is lovely."

Violanti didn't say anything more until he reached the door that would lead to his apartment. As the Madam turned to leave him, heading towards her own apartment but two doors down, he stopped her. "When she comes back you'll tell me?"

"Of course," she promised at once.

"Good. I want her. She is for me alone. Make sure the others know."

"They already do."

Violanti's eyes burned in response and it was the closing of the door that allowed her, at last, to break free from the dangerous, threatening power of his gaze.

Trembling, Delilah made for her door. It crossed her mind that perhaps the innocent Ms. Peters wasn't quite up to handling a man like Violanti. Not that it mattered, she realized. Once Violanti set his mind on something, it was impossible to deter him. Absolutely impossible.

Chapter Four

"Have you lost weight, Aerin?"

Aerin looked up from the coffee pot, where her hands were busy making that first, desperately needed, cup of liquid lightning. With a frown she found herself facing one of her numerous bosses—there were always more Chiefs than Indians in the company—a woman by the name of...Paula. Yes. It was Paula.

Paula had never spoken more than two words to her before...and certainly not in idle conversation.

"No. I don't think so," she said, finding her voice at last.

Paula's eyes were catty. Assessing. They darted from Aerin's round face to the plain leather pumps she wore, as if searching for something to find fault with but finding nothing. "Well you look...nice."

Aerin tried not to grimace at the woman's condescending tone. She didn't, in her heart, believe that Paula was deliberately insulting, so the woman's tone must be overlooked. Paula was simply used to being at the top of the food chain, it was no doubt quite unusual for her to converse with the prey. "Thank you," Aerin finally acknowledged, though her voice was little more than a murmur.

"I like what you've done with your hair," was Paula's last comment as she walked past the small break-room. No doubt as soon as Aerin was gone from her sight, she was also gone from her mind.

Aerin, shocked and surprised by the exchange, fingered the hair that fell to her neck. Frowning all the more, knowing full well she hadn't done anything different with her hair today than she had the day before, she finally let it drop back onto her collar. She shrugged. Perhaps Paula was merely trying to be nice, sociable.

Would wonders never cease?

Aerin giggled, then started, surprised by the sound.

Blushing over her own behavior, she drowned a lingering smile in her cup of coffee.

* * * * *

That day at lunch, Aerin was surprised to see a co-worker occupying her usual bench in the park. Instead of veering off and finding another secluded spot as she might normally have done, she decided to join the woman there.

"It's a lovely day," Aerin offered in way of greeting. "Mind if I sit?" She gestured to the space on the bench.

The woman smiled. "Sure, have a seat. Hey," she said with a dawning smile, "I know you. You work on rush print."

"Yeah. I'm the one they go to when they need a print job right away, unfortunately," Aerin chuckled, and was surprised at how easy the interaction was. The woman was perhaps a good ten to fifteen years younger and decidedly prettier. But for once Aerin didn't feel daunted by that fact. So the woman was slim and shapely, so she was young and free of wrinkles. It didn't matter. For once Aerin felt entirely at ease with what she saw as her own aesthetic deficiencies in the presence of someone who appeared to have none.

The woman shook her head. "I wouldn't want your job for the world. I work in receiving and order entry. We don't have to work under deadlines or strive to make production, thank goodness. The job's stressful enough as it is without all those burdens added to it."

"Well, you get used to it. I can't really remember what it was like before I started working in production. I used to be a proof reader," she explained, "until they transferred me to another department."

"I'm Heather Knowles," the woman introduced herself.

"Aerin Peters."

"I've worked here about six months and I think this is the first time I've ever really spoken so much with a co-worker," Heather laughed.

"That's the professional world for you," Aerin chuckled before she realized she was even going to, realizing she rarely *ever* spoke to co-workers if she could help it. "Ours is not a very sociable company, everyone kind of keeps to themselves around here. Actually, I think this is the first time in weeks that I've spoken more than two words to anyone myself."

"Good grief. Will it always be like this then?" The rueful grin on Heather's face transformed it, making her seem even younger. "'Cause I don't think I can live with that," she laughed outright then.

Aerin mused. "I think it is, most of the time. Actually, I think it's kind of a necessity in the corporate world. The only way to get a job done in a place like this is to keep socialization down to a minimum. One doesn't have time to make friends when one is too busy scurrying here or there, trying to make deadlines like a good worker bee." For the first time Aerin saw clearly that this was the case, at least in her own personal experience. Her very profession was one that limited her social interaction. Had she chosen such a path out of college deliberately, because she was so shy and introverted? She didn't know, not for sure.

Violanti would know.

Now why had *that* thought occurred to her?

Heather's words snapped her out of that odd confusion. "Well, we'll just have to agree to socialize with each other as often as possible then. Everyone needs friends, at work and at play. Who cares what the unspoken rules of the corporate world are?"

Aerin laughed again, easier this time because she wasn't so surprised by it. "I'd like that Heather. Very much."

Heather rose. "Well my break is past over. But I'll take tomorrow's lunch at twelve so we can spend the hour together. If you want to, that is."

"I'll be here." Aerin felt her heart swell with anticipation and hope. It would be nice to have a lunch partner.

"We can feed the ducks, if there are any."

"That would be lovely."

"Screw the professional world." Heather turned to leave, tossing a wave over her shoulder along with the jovial goodbye. "Later."

Aerin waved her off and ate with a gusto she hadn't felt in ages.

* * * * *

The next few days went by quickly. And Aerin couldn't have been happier for that boon. Thursday afternoon, while typesetting a template of several different wedding invitations, Aerin realized it had been a really good week. Possibly the best she'd had in years.

Aerin had been on top of her game this week. Being one of the fastest typists, she was often given a larger workload than many of her colleagues, a daunting list of tasks that never seemed to want to end. This week she had breezed right through the numerous business cards, wedding invitations, and award certificates she'd been assigned to lay out and typeset. She'd even met her demanding production goal and surpassed it, perhaps for the first time in six months.

Heather had met her every day for lunch in the park at twelve o'clock sharp, true to her word. For the first time in memory, Aerin had someone to talk to. Someone who she felt comfortable with. Someone who didn't seem to judge her on her looks, or on her too shy demeanor. They spoke of work, of mutual interests—books and music—and of hobbies. They had quite a lot in common, as well as quite a lot of differences. Aerin felt sure that they were becoming more than just co-workers sharing lunch. They were becoming good friends.

They would go shopping together this Sunday. Aerin looked forward to it with the hunger a starving animal might have for a raw steak. At times, she felt pitiful over that, but at others she didn't give a rat's ass how pathetic it might have seemed to an outsider. She had a new friend and for the first time in a long while it felt right.

She had Heather to thank for that. And Fetish. And…what had his name been? Violanti. Violanti, of course. That was it. What a horrible person she must be to struggle over something so simple, yet important, as the memory of his name. He'd given her the experience of a lifetime with his presence and his attention…and something else. She couldn't remember what. Her mind tried to shy away from the memory, but like an oil slick on the surface of the ocean it lingered.

How could she come so close to forgetting his *name*? After such an amazing night spent deep in eroticism, in conversation and in longing. What was wrong with her? She shook her head in an effort to clear it.

It was unforgivable enough that she couldn't distinctly remember the planes of his face. Or the color of his eyes. Hadn't the color of his eyes been incredible…surely the picture of them should have stayed clear in her mind? Were they brown? Green? Yes, perhaps that was the color. They had been green. Yes. She was sure of that now.

But wait.

No.

Green, jade-green, had been the color of the room they had shared. The room with the two-way mirror.

So what color were his eyes?

Squeezing her eyes tightly shut, she rubbed a hurried hand through her thick hair. Something wasn't right. How could she not remember him? She had a great memory, and even now she could remember the scent of that jade and cream room. Vanilla, interspersed with accents of sweet and tangy fruit. Her nose was practically filled with that perfume now as she imagined it.

But Violanti, his face and eyes—everything—was a blur in her memory. And come to think of it...so was the face of Madame Delilah. No matter how hard she struggled, she could not recall one detail of either Violanti's or the Madame's countenances.

Perhaps the fine Cristal champagne had gone to her head, affecting her much more strongly that she had realized at the time.

It made her more than a little sad that she couldn't remember every single nuance of her night at Fetish. It had been a grand adventure. Perhaps not exactly as she'd envisioned, but at the same time it had been far better than any imaginings she'd previously entertained. At least...she thought it had been a far better time...she couldn't be certain now. Too much was a blur. Too much had been forgotten.

Perhaps it wouldn't be so foolish on her part to go back there. One more time. Just once more, to find the reason why she was so certain it had been a liberating experience. Such a pleasure. Such a joy.

With a happy smile she was at last able to let go of her musings, and free to crank out the remainder of the waiting wedding invitations. Work was never so easy. Her fingers flew across the keys and her thoughts flew towards the weekend. Towards her visit to Fetish, and towards her shopping trip with her new friend. As always, she looked ahead to the weekend—*especially* Saturday—with eager anticipation. But this time for different reasons.

Different reasons entirely.

Chapter Five

"I'm glad to see you back, Aerin." Madame Delilah grasped Aerin's hands in hers and offered a kiss to each cheek.

"Me, too," she laughed, a little self-consciously.

"Violanti speaks highly of you. I must admit that this pleases me—our Violanti is not an easy man to impress. Not by far. Don't be surprised if he seeks you out again tonight. I certainly wouldn't be."

Aerin hoped he would. In fact, her account was going to be five thousand dollars poorer after tonight, because she was banking on it. "What did he say?"

Madame Delilah smiled enigmatically. "This and that...but I can tell from his tone that you both had a good time. I trust it was all you'd hoped for?"

"I came back didn't I?" Aerin almost giggled over her swift response. This was so unlike her, this feeling of daring and boldness that swam through her. The giggling was unlike her...in fact a lot of her actions had been alien to her this past week. How exciting.

"Indeed," the Madame laughed. "And the adventure seems to have done you much good. Why, I do believe there's a bit of color in your cheeks! And to think, a week ago you seemed near collapse you were so pale."

Aerin smiled easily enough, but was uncomfortable hearing such bald talk about her appearance, which was never much to be proud of even under the best of circumstances. "Perhaps it's the fresh spring air," she offered, finally.

"Perhaps." The Madame's eyes glittered above her smile. "You remember the rules?"

Though she hadn't really given them thought until that moment, Aerin *did* remember the club's rules. Clearly. "Yes. I remember."

"Good. Shall I charge to the same account?"

Aerin cringed — but only a little — reminded once again that this was a service she was paying for. Ah well, it was for the best, that reminder. She shouldn't read too much into Violanti's interest — or any one else's here for that matter. It was her money they were interested in really, nothing else. "The same, yes. Thank you."

"Good." The Madame's smile broadened, the stretch of her full lips making her noble, attractive face all the more handsome. "You can go on through," she motioned to the door that would lead to the common room of the club, "I believe you can find the way without my help."

"Thank you," Aerin murmured. Then, with a deep, steadying breath, she turned and entered through the door that would take her deeper into Fetish.

The corridor that led from the Madame's office to the wide, open space of the first sitting room was short and wide. It was decorated with a couple of large paintings, reproductions of pre-Raphaelite artists like Waterhouse or Rossetti from the look of them. They were lovely, and seemed dreamy and surreal to her eyes.

Dreamy and surreal. Both words were a perfect description for how she felt as she entered the common room, where a dozen or so clients already lounged with their escorts.

The room was a large, nearly circular construction, decorated in luxurious hues and fabrics. There were several doors, some were opened and some were closed. An open coupling of large oak doors leading out to a well-kept garden let in a nice, cool, night breeze. Oddly, there were no windows here, and where there appeared room and position for one, a giant tapestry or painting graced the wall instead.

There were four plain-fronted doors set in the walls— all of them were closed—and these led deeper into the bowels of the mansion. Violanti had led her through one of them on her last visit, taking her into the tiny hallway that would lead them to the Green door.

It seemed that behind most doors in this palace there lay a corridor to yet another door. And beyond that...Aerin wasn't sure.

In this room there was another set of double doors. These were exceptionally wide so that they nearly swallowed the breadth of the wall they were set into, and they had been opened to reveal another sitting room beyond it. That room was not unlike this one. Aerin knew, from her previous tour, that there were at least two other chambers like this one. Rooms in which the clients were free to roam about unattended...as they were not allowed to enter the doors leading to the inner sanctums without an escort.

There were rules here. Aerin sensed they were sacred ones, not to be broken. She wondered idly if there were bouncers in a place such as this, for surely there must be, somewhere. Though she'd yet to notice any. No doubt in the past at least one or two clients had tried to bend the rules and had been thrown out by the faceless security personnel.

And if not by bouncers then by something worse.

Now where did that thought come from, Aerin wondered? Of all things, Fetish did not seem to be a threatening place. Well…not entirely. Aerin shook her head to clear it. There was an undercurrent here of mystery and danger…but that sort of thing went hand and hand with a place like Fetish. There was nothing more to it than that. Surely.

Aerin felt the need for a quick dose of courage and reached for the nearest available glass of champagne — Cristal, as usual. It seemed the invisible owner of this place had a taste for the stuff, or knew his patrons would. She wondered what type of man could own and operate such an establishment as Fetish. What would he be like? Arrogant, sophisticated, spoiled, and filthy rich, most likely.

Her eyes swept the room, briefly meeting those of another patron, a dark-haired blue-eyed man dressed in jeans and a blazer. They nodded to each other, a polite gesture, and quickly looked away. Aerin raised her glass, throat dry. The drink was crisp and refreshing, chilled to perfection…but it was not enough to calm the trembles and quakes that continued to shake her composure.

"Back again, I see."

Aerin turned and found Violanti standing alarmingly close, though she hadn't even heard his approach. Her eyes rose up and up to meet his. She'd forgotten how tall he was. Among other things. His long black hair was thick and shimmering down about his shoulders. She'd forgotten just how soft it looked, but now the memories assailed her with the force of a storm wind blowing across the wastelands of her mind.

That hair had brushed across her skin like a thousand caressing fingers. With every move he'd made, so close to her that night, his hair had kissed her. His breath had kissed her. And where those two did not caress, he'd used his lips and fingers and honeyed words to assuage the loss.

It was her own prudish reluctance that had kept them from going further than their fully clothed touching. Well, she'd been fully clothed but he...he'd been scrumptiously disheveled after masturbating before her.

Masturbating...she remembered it all so clearly now, these things that should have been like detailed flames in her memories this past week. Gawd, he'd been so incredibly sexy, so unbelievably open and shameless with her. And she'd turned away from joining him in those moments? And from the invitation he'd offered after?

What a fool she'd been.

With a jerk she knew was visible she tore herself back to his softly rumbled greeting. "Yeah, I'm back," she said lamely.

"So I see." That smile of his — part mockery, part humor, all sensuality — was a sweet memory all its own. How could she have forgotten all of this? "May I share company with you, Mistress?"

She snorted, her hands flying up to late cover the sound she couldn't contain. What was wrong with her? She wasn't usually so emotive, was always too busy hiding herself in the crowd, trying to avoid notice. Controlling herself, but barely, she lowered her hands and swallowed a panicked laugh.

"I thought we were beyond the Mistress thing. Or...don't you remember my name?" It wouldn't be forgivable of him; after all, she'd forgotten his a half-dozen times over the past week.

His smile broadened, revealing a blaze of strong, white teeth. His parents must have paid a fortune in braces for such a smile. She winced mentally at the thought; even in her mind she was showing her age. It came from being older than her escort, she supposed, though she'd tried until now not to dwell on it much.

But how old was he, really? She couldn't have said, though she did feel older and was quite certain she was. But...? Violanti was possessed of the kind of face that held an ageless quality. He could be in his mid to late twenties...he could be nearer to forty, though she doubted it. It was his eyes, more than anything else, that gave him a sort of greater age. They seemed to be ancient, worldly, and very knowing. He would look only slightly different in his dotage, of this she had no doubt. His impeccable breeding and his clearly exotic heritage would see to that.

"I remember everything, Aerin." He reached out, offering her his hand, palm up. Like a gallant knight begging his lady for a favor. His hair moved again, revealing a quick glimpse of the silver talon piercing his ear lobe. "Will you come with me, or no? I have much to show you tonight, if you would be with me."

Her heart warmed and she forgot to be cautious. "What will you show me?" She gave him her hand, felt it enveloped by that cool, hard strength.

"Everything, if you'll allow me." His eyes—those glorious, magical eyes—shimmered with their ever-changing color.

A hot shiver raced down her spine. A primitive warning sounded its call in her deepest heart. It was swiftly discarded, far too swiftly for her to take heed. Her escort was too potently sexual for her to care for or even really take note of such warnings.

He pulled her close to his side, openly inhaled her scent, and closed his eyes as if in bliss. "You're headier than wine, do you know that?"

Her breath bubbled into a soft, nervous laugh. He had a way with words that was both disarming and thrilling.

"I'll grow drunk off you if I'm not careful," he teased. Clearly it must be teasing. This was what he did for a living, after all, teasing and titillating older women. "And already I know that one taste of you is not enough for a glutton such as I."

"You don't need that silver tongue with me," she said with a smile, though she did so love his flirting. It was just that she felt there was something more to this play, something she didn't quite understand, and it made her more than a little uncomfortable. She was out of her league and knew it, not that it mattered much this far into the game.

"Oh, but you've yet to know the full pleasure of my silver tongue, Mistress." The twinkle in his eyes was both wicked and hot. "Perhaps, before this night is over, you'll feel differently about it."

It was nearly impossible to hold at bay the girlish giggle that tickled the back of her throat, demanding release. But somehow she managed. *Good grief, what is wrong with me lately?* She hadn't the faintest idea.

And the hell with it, she didn't care. She was, in fact, having the best damn time of her life.

"What have you got planned for this evening?" she asked, surprised at how easy this byplay was between them. She would be content to do pretty much anything he asked tonight. The thought of what he might ask, what he would likely ask, made her shiver delicately with anticipation.

He chuckled, his long black hair spilling out about his shoulders and arms. She'd forgotten how long it was. And with his small movement, the scent of him reached her, conquered her, drugged her senses. Cinnamon and almond and his own unique perfume; it was a delicious, sinful combination. Her womb felt heavy, hot, and tight with a desperate longing. "Pleasure. Always pleasure with you, Aerin my sweet."

He took her hand in a firmer grip and led her through the room, to one of the doors set into the walls. This door opened before him, as if automated, and closed silently behind them. They were in another room now, a small sort of sitting room, decorated with a small couch, chair and ottoman. There was a lone door set in the wall, nothing else. Its color was a deep royal blue, and Aerin had a strong compulsion to open it and see what lay beyond the azure barrier.

"As you know, Fetish caters to the hedonistic urges of its clients. Here any pleasure can be found, though sexual pleasures are, of course, more popular than any other, and expected." From his great height towering above her, he bent his head and pressed a chaste kiss atop her head before pulling back and staring at the door before them with a pensive look.

"The last time you were here, I learned a great deal about who you are. About your desires and longings, though you tried so hard to hide them." He sounded disappointed in that, but continued in his deep and lilting voice. "I have an almost certain idea of what you would like to gain from your visits here. Of what will bring you the most pleasure. But I must give you a choice before I take control of this situation. Before I can better guide you on your journey."

"What do you mean?" she frowned.

He turned fully to her, tilting her head up with a finger beneath her chin, so that their eyes met. The color of his irises changed with dizzying rapidity. "You can choose many different paths to explore here, more than you can imagine. You should know what they are before we go farther. I feel that I know you well enough to guide you from here, but I could be wrong. I will not take the chance and ruin your enjoyment of this place."

"Go on," she urged, curious.

"Our clients tell us what they want and we make their wishes come true. It's our purpose. But you are different, you are more reserved. In fact, I don't think you really know what you want beyond happiness, that intangible yet incredibly powerful state of being. Happiness you'll get, I promise that, but a taste of adventure is what I most want to give you. So for you there will be a journey, from a shy and untouched innocent to—I hope—a sultry and confident woman who knows and delights in every aspect of her sensuality. Both as a person, and a lover, in equal measure. I would guide you on that journey. But as I said before, I will ask you your preferences first.

"We have many rooms in this place, as I'm sure you've guessed by now. And inside each one there will be a different world of pleasure to be discovered. For you, I have chosen rooms that, I feel, are best suited to arousing your deepest sensual being. But there are rooms that are also suited to arouse your curiosity and...other things. I would avoid those this early into your journey, though I will ask you now what your preferences are, as they are the most important."

He smiled that secretive, satyr's smile of his and things deep in her breasts and belly tightened and yearned. "Our name is not Fetish merely because of whimsy. If you were to enter all the doors in this place you would eventually have seen every deviant's fantasy come to life and more. For you, I choose the softer, more feminine aspects of Fetish, because I believe you are soft and feminine through and through.

"But, if you should will it, I will take you upon a different road. I can show you latex fetishes, medical fetishes, stomping fetishes, blood fetishes…everything you could possibly imagine. If you asked me now, I could take you to a room that caters only to those interested in elaborate rope bondage scenarios. I could take you to a room where pain is the greatest catalyst for pleasure. Or I could take you to a room where anal congress is most dearly sought after, rough and gentle, and all that is in between. Here, there are endless possibilities."

She shied away from the scope and imagination of the club…she'd never given thought to how far the establishment might go towards pleasing it's customers sexually. She'd assumed much…but not so much.

She'd been assured, more than once, that the escorts here did only what they wanted to do with the clients. If there were extreme fetishes being catered to within the club's walls, she felt sure it was with mutual consent of those involved and reminded herself of that now. "What," she swallowed, "what fetish have you chosen for me tonight?"

He grinned wide, showing his too-bright teeth again. "Not so much a fetish in the sense of the word you might assume. For you I would say your fetish is an object of reverence, an intangible thing that requires attention and devotion and utmost care. Your inner sensuality. It sleeps now, but only lightly after your last visit, I think. I would like to awaken this deep place inside of you. I would like to see you blossom as you were meant to. I want to see you ripe, open, and drunk upon your own power as a woman."

All traces of self-confidence vanished as if they had never been. She winced at the sudden loss and breathed harshly, nervously. "You talk as if I'm some dull spinster."

"Don't you see yourself thus," his words were merciless, demanding, "I would not believe you if you said otherwise, nor do I think you would lie about so serious a thing."

"And I don't think you can make me see myself any differently." She avoided the admission that she did, indeed, see herself as he'd suggested.

"Do you not?" His eyes changed color most rapidly now, silver and green and blue and back again. The colors seemed so deep as to be pools of liquid beneath the long dark fan of his lashes. "Have you not already felt a change within yourself, after only one evening here with me?"

She had. But how could he know that? Had it been that obvious? "Yes," she admitted, never thinking to lie, not to this man who would doubtless have sensed the lie before she'd finished mouthing it. He was far too astute, far too knowing, to attempt any sort of subterfuge. "I have felt different. I don't know how, but I have." Her hands trembled, one still held captive by his.

"Then trust me to know that together, we can awaken your deepest self. If you should choose to explore the world of Fetish then I will be glad to accompany you. But I believe that I can lead us both on this journey. Trust me to know what steps to take and I promise you that you will never regret that trust."

Though she was curious to see the strange rooms he'd mentioned, she knew she was less apt to gain any sort of lasting benefit from what she might find there. What Violanti spoke of now was liberation, of her self, of her sensuality, of her very womanhood. If he could bring about such a wonder, if he could set her free—free to be herself in every way—she would be forever grateful.

He'd already wrought such a welcome change in her that she could hardly believe it. She would trust him a little more, now, if only because he asked it of her. "Lead the way, Violanti. I trust you," she smiled, an honest smile, and was relieved that she didn't feel at all self-conscious about it.

His eyes darkened, a dangerous storm brewed in their depths, electrifying her with the intensity of his gaze. "Good. I need that trust, Aerin. More than you know." He led her to the blue door, his hand cool and strong around hers. "Now let me guide you. Let me bring you. Let me show you how much of a woman you really are."

Chapter Six

The blue door opened and, not surprisingly, the room beyond was decorated in various hues of azure, turquoise, and royal blue. It was a calming, soothing décor, cool and inviting. Every aspect was meant to draw an occupant inward, deeper into the sea of color and—of course—texture. Brocades, silks—both raw and refined, satins, cottons, and velour adorned every available surface. It was truly lovely. Aerin sighed, relaxing deeply and immediately into the plush atmosphere of the room.

There was a bed in the center of the space, raised on three marble steps so that it was the main attraction of the room. Rich draperies hung from the immense posters of the bed's frame, in various shades of blue, silver, white, and cream. The floor was tiled with tiny pieces of polished marble and granite. The cold hard aspect of such an unforgiving material was softened by numerous thickly piled fur rugs, each a decadent and sinful expense of luxury and refined taste.

There were no windows, but the walls were covered with carvings and paintings the likes of which Aerin—a voracious art lover herself—had never seen. This artwork belonged in a palace, or museum, not a Seattle mansion. Her fingers fairly itched to reach for one of the paintings. She'd have given her soul to own but one, they were so fine.

She tore her attention away from the art—it was almost painful—and looked around, noting the similarities and differences of this room and the jade one she'd occupied on her first visit. "No two-way mirrors this time?" she asked with a small, teasing smile.

He returned it with one of his own. "I wanted your undivided attention tonight, so no, I'm afraid there are no two-way mirrors this time."

He led her, at once, directly to the bed. She balked, hesitant and nervous about his intentions. He glanced at her; a hot, warning look in his mercurial eyes. "Are you already withdrawing your trust, Aerin? So soon?"

"N-no," she said, then more firmly, "no. Of course not. I'm just a little nervous, that's all." And it was the truth, but not entirely. Yes she was nervous, but she was also excited. Very excited about what would come next.

"Good. I'd hate for you to be so hasty as that, when I have such a lovely evening planned for the both of us."

"And what exactly do you have planned?" she was moved to ask.

He sat her down upon the edge of the bed and joined her, drawing so close that the scent of him enveloped her in a warm cloud. "So much, I don't even know where to begin. For tonight, there will be much pleasure — for both of us, but I don't want to rush it. I want to savor every nuance of your self-discovery."

"I'm not ready to sleep with you," she admitted in a rush.

His eyes widened, then fell shuttered beneath thick lashes. "I never said anything about sleep."

"Don't tease. I-I like you a lot Violanti, but I'm not going to let you be a prostitute for me…"

His cool hand clamped over her mouth, silencing her. His face was hardened, dangerous, a warning. "Don't ever speak of that again. You keep coming back to this and I am tiring of it. I am no whore. Nor are you. Leave it, you silly woman. Leave it be."

She scowled at him over his hand and moved to bite him — shocking even herself at so bold and action.

Violanti only grinned as her teeth nicked him, his smile wolfish this time, before lowering his hand. "There'll be time for that later, sweet," he promised devilishly.

Aerin was more than a little titillated by his words, her knees felt weak as water.

"For now, I will tell you that tonight we will continue your journey by exploring touch. The need and desire for touch, both giving and receiving. I think I will give you dominion and allow you to explore the giving end of this venture first. Though I ache most fiercely to touch you, I think you need this small taste of supremacy so soon in our relationship."

She felt her hands tingle — actually tingle — with the urge to touch him. But she fought the urge and won, barely. She didn't want to seem too eager. Though in truth she was very, *very* eager.

"Are you ready Aerin? The night will linger but so long, even for lovers such as you and I are about to become."

Now she wasn't too sure about that, though she supposed they were already lovers of a sort. How incredible that so lovely, so perfect, so dangerously sexy a man like Violanti could even speak of being her lover. And she had the wondrous idea that he sincerely meant every word. She'd never been happier, not even close.

"I'm ready," she murmured, wondering that such a sultry voice could belong to her; overjoyed when she realized fully that it did.

"Undress me, sweet Aerin," he commanded in a whisper that stroked over her skin like the brush of invisible lips.

Her hands shook as she brought them to the hem of his skin-tight, black t-shirt. He accommodatingly raised his arms above his head as she lifted it, allowing her to expose the long length of his tightly muscled stomach and chest. The neck of the shirt came free of his head, but she was too short to lift it free of his arms so he finished the job for her, tossing the dark cloth carelessly to the floor.

Her eyes drank him up, from his corded neck, to his alarmingly broad shoulders, to his rounded pectorals and washboard abs. His left nipple—dark brown against the hairless chest—was pierced by a tiny silver loop. His warm-hued olive skin was cooled somewhat by the blue of the room, but she felt overcome with heat all the same. He was sheer perfection, beyond any she could have imagined or dreamed. And for the moment he was all hers. *Hers!* It was unbelievable.

She reached out to touch his glinting nipple ring, to run her hands down that gorgeous expanse of muscled chest, and gasped when he captured her questing hands in a firm grip with but one of his own.

"Not yet," his gaze seared her. "I couldn't take that, not so soon. For now, give me your glasses before they slip off your face." She did, though her vision was so blurry without them she could barely see him. He took them and laid them on a convenient table by the bed, before turning back to her. "Now. Undress me before we go any further.

Now. Undress me," he finished in another whisper before gently releasing her.

Her hands fluttered down to his belt buckle, careful not to even brush against the lure of his sensual skin. But oh, how badly she wanted to touch. How desperately she longed for it. She gritted her teeth and was startled when Violanti chuckled, having heard the telltale sound from within her mouth.

Their eyes met, his scorching her to her soul. There was a promise there, a secret knowledge in those depths, a dark and heady knowledge that only a lover could have. And hadn't she admitted that they were already lovers—if not of the flesh, then of the mind? She'd longed for this advance in their relationship. It would do her no good to lie to herself about the truth of it. She wanted him for a lover, for her first lover. If he wanted them joined tonight, she would not deny him. Or herself.

His belt buckle was of heavy silver—he seemed to have his own fetish for silver—and she was amazed that her quaking hands managed to undo the fastening. The button fly of his black vinyl pants came next, and he leaned back on his elbows to aid her efforts. The ridge of his arousal was large, hard, and warm as her fingers unavoidably brushed over it in her bid to loosen his pants. Her heart thundered. Her sex ached, swelled, and flooded with arousal. Her breath came in soft pants of air that fluttered over her lips and out towards his skin.

It seemed as if her very breath longed to stroke over him, to touch him.

He wasn't wearing any underclothing. The swell of his cock fell free of its confines, heavy and thick onto her hands as she unfastened the last of his buttons. Her hands faltered and her breath caught. She'd never touched a man thus. Her gaze darted up to clash with his. The fire of desire blazed between them, burning brighter than ever.

"Finish it, sweet," he instructed softly. "The touching will come after, I promise. All you want and more."

Desperate now, she tugged at the loosened waistband of his pants. He lifted his hips, thrusting that smooth column of sex up towards her face as she bent forward with her efforts. The scent of him, more concentrated here at the core of his masculinity, swamped her. Her mouth watered. His natural perfume filled her nose and lungs, and she was so drunk with lust she might have died from it.

But not before she had him fully naked. How could she die without first seeing such a vision to comfort her in her last waking moments before sinking deep into death's ebony blanket?

Awkward but determined, she slid from the bed, worked to remove his calf-high boots, and then pushed his pants down to his ankles, kneeling on the floor between his legs as she moved to accomplish the task. Once the clothing was removed — at last! — she looked up at him and stilled. Her face was level with his cock. That long, hard staff of rigid tissue, engorged with blood, aroused for her.

Aerin felt rather than heard the tiny, mewling noise that escaped from the depths of her throat. His legs spread wider before her, the delicious cinnamon and almond scent of him growing stronger, as he shifted to allow her a better view.

"Can you doubt how much I want you now, Aerin?"

She swallowed and shook her head, her eyes moving of their own volition to drink him in as she knelt between his thighs.

"Do you desire me?"

She hesitated and then nodded, for it was the most honest truth she knew in that moment.

"Then feel no regrets. None. Now. Touch me. Please touch me."

Her hands, visibly trembling with her nervousness and excitement, swept up to rest against his knees. It was her eyes that touched him more freely, from head to chest, belly to sex, to his legs and — *oh, how unexpectedly beautiful* — his feet.

"Touch me everywhere," he encouraged.

Her hands petted the soft down of his leg hair, from his knees to his calves then back up to his thighs. Never once did her hands separate from his dusky flesh, never once did she look away. He was too beautiful for words, too sexy for thought.

Her body trembled; her breath came in unsteady pants that she knew he could hear.

"What are you thinking," he asked in a gentle whisper that breathed across her face like a softly scented breeze.

Could she find the words to convey her wonder? Did those words exist in the human vocabulary? She would try and hope not to taint the moment with her inadequate speech. "Y-you smell so good," her voice shook, cushioned — or choked — by the husky breaths that entered her words. "And I've never..." she faltered. "I've never touched anything so fine," her hands brushed over his thighs once more as she finished.

"Touch all of me. Feel more of me." He lay back with a deep, unsteady draw of breath.

"Yes," she breathed.

Avoiding his cock, though she desperately longed to touch him there, she rose slowly until she was half leaning, half lying over him, trailing her hands up his body. She raised her hands to his shoulders. His skin was cool, as cool as the room, which was unexpected—though she realized in the back of her mind that he was always this cool—and smooth as the finest silk. Silk over steel, for his muscles were even harder than they looked beneath his skin.

She tested those muscles, squeezing him firmly, as firmly as she wanted to squeeze other things. Next her hands roved over the broad planes of his chest. The glint of the silver nipple ring fascinated her. When she dared to touch it, to gently tug upon it, Violanti hissed and his chest swelled beneath her hands.

Jerking her hands back, unnerved by the sound, she moved to sit beside him again, feeling her breath escape her in a rush. Violanti immediately countered her move, capturing her hands, bringing them back flush with his chest. "Do that again," he begged—commanded—pleaded.

She tugged gently upon the ring, eyes roving over him, unable to miss the pulse that shook his rigid member when she did so, even with her poor eyesight. Repeating the gesture, her eyes widened to see the response echoed once more in the swelling tissues of his cock. His perfume teased her again, drugging her, arousing her ever more.

Daring more than ever now, she leaned forward and licked the pierced nipple. Violanti groaned, a hand flying forward to tangle in her hair. She repeated the caress, this time suckling him as well as licking him, though his nipple was flat and somewhat hard to draw upon even pierced as it was. Violanti's hips bucked and his fist tightened against her scalp.

Aerin had never felt as strong as she did then, with her lover's powerful body held captive to even so slight a caress as this.

Her hair fell in a heavy curtain about her face as she moved back over him and bent to press her lips more tightly to his warming flesh. In the very deepest recesses of her mind she wondered that her hair could feel heavy, it had always been lank and thin, but that thought was buried too deep for her to really give it proper notice.

And there were so many more important things demanding her notice at the moment.

Like the thick corded muscles of his throat. Feeling no resistance in him, Aerin lifted her lips to it, pressing against that flesh with a greedy force. Violanti's breath exploded in her ear.

"Bite me there," he said in a shaky voice that she'd never heard him use before, "*please.*"

Without thinking twice she did, gently at first, but when Violanti pushed her mouth tighter against his throat with that fist still tangled in her hair, she bit harder. He groaned, a loud noise that nearly startled her it was so masculine, so full of arousal and hunger and heat.

"Harder," he demanded pulling her body against his so that they fell back together onto the bed.

She bit harder, drawing his skin into her mouth, knowing she would leave a love mark and reveling in that potent knowledge.

The strong frame of his body shuddered beneath her, the swell of his cock prodding her stomach demandingly. "Harder, please, harder, do it Aerin!"

Any harder and she would have drawn blood. So she drew back, rising over him so that her chestnut hair fell forward and tangled with his indigo black strands. Their eyes met. She could have sworn that his were tinged with red, so powerful was his need in that moment.

Nearly as powerful as hers.

"Touch me all over, Aerin. I need you," his hands fisted up at his temples, clear evidence of his growing need and frustration. His words intoxicated her, seduced her, ensorcelled her.

She straddled him as he lay there, feeling no shame or awkwardness in it as she might have done but a few moments earlier. Something had changed between them. Some exchange of power, of supremacy had occurred, though Aerin had no idea why she felt it had. It just had. Violanti was in thrall to her, to her power as a woman, in a way she never would have—could have—believed. He wanted her. Truly and unashamedly, he wanted her.

Well she wanted him too. And she meant to have him.

But for now, the touching. The touching he seemed to need, to crave from her.

Her hands swept over his chest and stomach. The muscles of his belly clenched, as if tickled, and she repeated the caress with a smile. To find such bliss in touching—she never would have imagined it possible—and again she was struck with the certainty that she'd never been happier than she was in this moment. With this man.

There was beauty in touch. She was a little surprised to realize that truth. A simple beauty that was innocent despite the very sexual nature of their situation. He was at once smooth and rough, hard and soft, in the way only a truly masculine male at the height of his sexual prime could be. His cock, hot now between her legs, burned her with incessant demand, and she shifted upon him instinctively.

Violanti groaned gutturally beneath her in answer to her movement upon him. "I can't take much more of this," he chuckled ruefully, and sounded more than a little surprised by the admission.

Her hands rose up and kneaded the ridges of his pectoral muscles, which were tight with a growing tension that was echoed in all the other planes of his body. The silver loop prodded against her palm and she nudged it, twisting it carefully in his flesh until he hissed, bucked up — nudging her off him — and rolled to cover her.

The shifting colors of his gaze hypnotized her, drawing her deep. His breath shuddered out of his mouth and down over her lips. His teeth looked sharp and wicked as he gritted them, his muscled jaw working tensely. Dark, dangerous intensity locked his muscles tight as his weight bore her deep into the mattress. Some hidden threat she couldn't name seemed to flow from him to her. Her instincts screamed at her to flee, that something was amiss, that something was terribly wrong, but *what* that was she couldn't have guessed. Then the unnamed moment passed and he eased atop her, that devil's smile coming to play about the corners of his mouth as if it had never left.

"You've learned this game too well, I think, and too quickly. Perhaps you're too much of a woman for me after all," he teased, clearly not meaning a word of it.

"I like touching you," she blurted out.

His eyes darkened and the danger was back. "And I like you touching me, sweet Aerin." His lashes curtained his eyes and his head lowered.

His lips were like the gentle graze of satin over hers. His breath tasted of cinnamon, filling her mouth as his lips gently parted hers. The warmth of his tongue licked tenderly into her mouth, tracing the outline of her lips and teeth. Widening her mouth eagerly to his kiss, she felt the brush of his tongue across her and moaned.

That he could have such a wonderful flavor was beyond her most fevered imaginings. Their tongues licked, again and again, as his thrust in and out of her mouth until she felt emboldened enough to follow his lead. Her hands rose up to entwine about his neck, the exquisite softness of his hair teasing her fingers and palms as they locked together, pulling him closer.

His teeth scraped over her lips, drawing one tiny dot of blood. She winced. He licked the blood away immediately and the pain was gone. The growl that escaped his lips then, bloomed into her mouth and she swallowed it, making it a part of her. His teeth scraped again, sharply, and everything went hazy and dark.

The bottom of the earth seemed to open up beneath them. Dizziness assailed her, disorientation and confusion overtook her. She felt his mouth on hers, drawing her bottom lip into his mouth. She felt the increasing heat of his skin against her clothed body, beneath her hands which had begun to stroke down over the length of his back and—oh heavens!—his tight buttocks. All else had faded. The only real and tangible thing in her world during that moment was Violanti. And Violanti's devastating kiss.

At once he drew back, a nearly violent shove that brought him towering back above her, and she came back to herself with a thud. His mouth was swollen, red, his eyes shifting colors with a violent swiftness. His body shuddered upon hers, his sex a hot brand against her stomach.

Moaning, beyond mere need or want, and feeling something far, far greater than the two combined, she sought to pull him back to her. She tugged demandingly on the length of his ebony hair. He shuddered again, but came back to her willingly, eyes nearly closed so heavy were his lids.

But instead of returning to her mouth, as she so longed for him to do, he buried his face in her neck. His breaths came harshly, vibrating the both of them as he lay back upon her. His mouth pressed like a hot brand into her throat, the ridge of his teeth behind them making his kiss hard and rough against her.

The strength of his hands held her upper arms in a vice-grip. Aerin felt his cock grind against her pubic bone and she eagerly opened her legs to bring him flush against the heart of her. She wrapped her legs around his hips, locking her ankles together, and moaned when he rolled his hips against her.

She felt the bite of his teeth against her a second before he pulled back again, this time with a roar that should have frightened her, but only served to enflame her more. He set himself back, drawing her up so that she sat beside him once more.

"We must slow down," his voice was unsteady, but he quickly regained his composure. His gaze burned across her face and body. "I haven't had my turn yet, sweet."

His hands were immediately at her throat, unbuttoning her demure blouse. The creamy linen was quickly and efficiently discarded, following the path of his own shirt so that it spilled like a cloud onto the floor. His eyes ate her, wide and hot, like flickering flames of silver, green, blue, and sometimes red.

"You're perfect," he breathed. Aerin almost believed the sincerity of his words, but her low self-image was too ingrained.

At last she could not doubt his sincerity, for when his hands reached out to her they shook almost violently. Broad palms cupped her breasts through the serviceable white satin of her bra. They lifted and tested the weight of her, thumbs gently stroking over the jut of her nipples through the material.

Looking at his face she saw first wonderment, awe, and then reverence. He truly seemed enthralled with the sight of her breasts. Truly appeared to find her, well, *attractive*.

Aerin swore to thank every lucky star that shone in the sky for this moment.

His fingers slipped—eager—moving to lower the straps of her bra. They swept around and behind her, artfully undoing the catch with but a flick of his fingers. His palms stroked down her back, slow, as if to better savor the feel of her skin.

The bra fell away, leaving her completely exposed.

His eyes drank her in.

Her nipples felt like diamonds on the tips of her breasts, which were heavy with desire. *Touch me*, her mind and body both screamed, *touch me there*, please. And then he did, as if he'd heard her demands. Or perhaps he'd wanted it as much as she. His hands took her, the weight of her filling them to overflowing, her nipples stabbing into his palms.

"Perfect," he murmured. His fingers stroked, plucking at her nipples, tugging and twisting them until she felt her back bow up towards the caress demandingly. "Beyond perfect," he amended.

Firmly now, his hands plumped her. Pressing her down until she lay back into the feather pillows on the bed. His hands wandered down, across the soft swell of her stomach and down to the tiny zipper of her green skirt. Seconds only and the skirt was gone, swept down her thighs and legs and tossed over the edge of the bed.

Aerin had daringly ignored her usual use of panty hose with the skirt while dressing for the night, opting instead for a risqué pair of thigh highs, creamy white to match her blouse, with tiny bows at the tops. She was ever so glad she had, when she saw the blatant appreciation stamped across Violanti's features once he'd caught sight of them. When he reverently kissed the tops of the stockings she almost fainted with the shock and pleasure, and vowed never to wear anything beneath her skirts but thigh highs for the rest of her life.

Her panties flew from her as if they had wings, his fingers easily hooking them and pulling them down her legs. His eyes burned her, his hands holding her legs spread wide to his gaze. A single, glittering drop of sweat trailed down his temple.

"I need you, Aerin," his eyes left her sex and met hers, "can you understand that? Forget the lesson, forget the plan, I *need* you."

She nodded, feeling the weight of the situation as if it were a palpable thing, though she didn't understand it.

"Give me all of you, sweet. I swear I'll keep and hold you safe. Just please don't pull back now," he groaned eyes roving back down over her body. "Please."

As if she could have pulled back. "I won't," she promised.

He spread her legs wider, more demanding now. She felt some shyness at being so displayed before him, but it was miniscule in the face of his obvious desire. They were nude together now, but for her stockings. For the first time in Aerin's life, she was nude before a man, ready to take him as her lover.

One of his hands moved between her legs. The touch of his fingers upon her downy hair, upon her wet and swollen flesh, made her squeal in surprised pleasure. Those fingers spread the folds of her cunt, opening the seam of her so that her deepest treasures were open to his gaze. "Sugar girl," he murmured, thrilling her.

His fingers stroked over her quim, smearing and spreading her moisture over every inch of quivering flesh that was open and blooming for his pleasure. His hair fell over his face, shielding him from her, giving him secrets and shadows. Those eyes of his glinted red beneath that curtain of hair for a moment, she could have sworn to it, then blazed a hard silver.

"Touching is important in this journey," he said. "So is tasting."

His body lowered. His head bent, his breath sent a scalding wave over her pussy, and then his mouth closed upon her.

Aerin screamed, nearly bucking him off of her.

He smiled against her, she could actually feel the curve of his lips there, and then they opened so that his tongue could dance against her. Never in a million years had Aerin expected this, and it was just as crazy and magical and exciting as she would have dreamed it had she dared. She flew, the world spun like a mad top around her, and all because Violanti's head was bobbing between her legs as he licked her from anus to clit and back again. Over and over until she thought she might die with the swelling excitement.

Now his mouth clamped upon her, sucking her. Wet noises filled the room and her ears, along with the sound of her frantic breaths and moans. She bucked up against his face and he pressed deeper into her, sucking and licking harder.

Then came the nibbles, the love bites, the sting of his teeth. She cried out, spreading her legs farther apart, begging with her body that he continue, that he never stop. There came a greater sting as he bit harder into her before he abruptly pulled away.

But, to her never-ending ecstasy, he replaced his mouth with his fingers. Thrusting his long middle finger deep into her pussy, filling and stretching her, while another finger played artfully with her swollen clit.

His eyes met hers as his hand thrust between her legs. "Sugar girl. Sweet. So fucking sweet." He licked his swollen, sultry lips that shone with her moisture.

The weight of his body covered her, his hand still moving deeply in and out of her cunt. Wet slapping noises accompanied his every motion. His mouth sealed against hers, and she tasted herself there on his lips and tongue. The kiss trailed away from her mouth to her jaw and throat. Then came a sharp sting and again the world went fuzzy and strange.

A feeling of warmth, liquid and thick, spread from her throat to his mouth which worked against her as his kiss deepened. The sensation of giving, of sharing something deep inside of her—something more than mere sex— welled up within her. In that moment she wanted nothing more than to disappear into Violanti, to give him all of her until there was nothing left.

The world spun wildly and turned gray around them. Violanti was the only solid thing in that strange reality. The single finger in her pussy became two, stretching her as he thrust his hand, hard, against her. A fingertip pressed into the hard button of her clit, once, twice, and on the third attempt she felt a flood of moisture rain down upon his hand. Her body became a living pulse, a giant throbbing heartbeat. And then she truly flew.

Her climax crashed down around her and she screamed louder than ever before. No release had ever taken her like this. Another finger moved into her and another until she felt she would be split open. It was as if Violanti was reaching for the very heart of her by way of her womb, he thrust so deeply into her.

The muscles of her cunt clamped down on his pounding hand until she was certain it caused him some pain. She felt so tight. So full of pleasure and passion and—yes—pain, for she was stretched wide and Violanti's mouth still drew upon her. The hand thrust deep into her again, hooking, curving inside of her until she felt a new sensation that was perhaps even more powerful than the climax that still gripped her.

She came again and again and again, screaming and crying and sobbing and moaning until she knew her voice was failing her. As was her vision...as were her lungs...until all went gray.

* * * * *

It was far too soon, for them both, and he knew it. But some strange fever had overtaken his better judgment and his self-control had slipped dangerously. He hungered so very deeply. His body and soul thirsted, his veins begged and yearned with their burning need. He was powerless against his own dark nature. Violanti sank his fangs sharply into her silken throat and drank deep.

Starlight exploded in every fiber of his being. So pure, so sweet. Her aura, a glowing golden halo that surrounded her at all times, extended to enfold him. Her life's energy as well as her blood filled him, fed him. She was so giving. So full of life. He'd never felt such wonder, such fulfillment, such ecstasy. And there was no hesitancy in her. She gave everything of herself to him, and through their open hearts he shared with her the gift that was his alone to give.

He was an incubus and a vampire, but these labels, these names were not so dark a curse as the modern world proclaimed. He had gifts unimagined, and used them now, to thank her for such a wonderful gift as her trust. She must trust him, for he could never have fed off her so fully if she'd been guarded or unwilling.

So innocent and yet so generous, that was his sweet Aerin through and through. The taste of her blood filled his mouth, made his head swim with spectacular visions of love and lust and desire. The flavor of her aura, her life essence, filled his body to overflowing until it sang with a vibrating energy the likes of which he hadn't felt in all his long years. Nothing had ever felt so unbelievably perfect.

He would never have enough of her. Not now, not ever.

He was out of his mind with love for her.

If there had ever been a time he had thought to bind her to him for his own pleasure, he now knew it was impossible. She had beaten him to it, binding him to her in a way he hadn't even known humans were capable of. He was instantly addicted. There would never be a moment, no matter how long he existed, of rest from wanting her. Needing her.

The explosion of her climax rocked him. He swallowed more of her. Gods! She filled every empty place within him. Through her he could see the sunlight, smell the spring flowers, feel the soft rain of morning dew. It had never been like this for him during a feeding.

Because this was no feeding. This was something else, something he had no name for.

He swallowed the hot, spicy taste of her again, his teeth vibrating with the pulse of her heart. The bright glow of her faded a bit as her strength flowed into him. She was growing weak, limp in his arms. He'd feared this. Had pulled back from biting her half a dozen times already, knowing it might come to this. He had no self-control with her, it was crazy to hope for any. She made him lose all discipline by merely looking at him with her incredible, bottomless eyes.

He had taken too much.

He swallowed one last time, unable to deny that last, deep sip, then released her. Putting her from him firmly, he looked her over to be sure he hadn't caused any lasting harm. Her aura brightened almost immediately. She was strong. She would be fine.

But would he? His head swam drunkenly. His entire body tingled within and without. The taste of her beckoned him for more, until he gritted his teeth against the powerful urge to drink from her again. The razor sharp edge of his fangs drew blood from his own lips and he tasted her there in his bloodstream with a broken cry. So sweet! So perfect. He was lost.

The soft silk of her skin eased his bloodlust, but awakened another. She moved against him with a soft moan, and the burning wet core of her sweet pussy brushed against him with her efforts. His hands were covered with the flood of her climax and he licked them, leaving pink stains of their mingled blood behind.

The dramatic slopes and curves of her body made his stomach clench and his heart beat a mad staccato in his chest. Her nipple tasted sweet, her breast and belly and navel were soft and perfect. He kissed her from head to toe, pausing to lick her behind the knees, to gently bite the tender skin of her ankles.

Touching his fill while she lay dazed in her swoon, he gave her the power that was his to share through that touch. A power that would sing through her, even if she had no idea what to do with it or how to use it. And she wouldn't. For now, the spell that protected Fetish would serve to dim her memory so that even if he told her, explained everything in detail, she would forget. But it would be there, that power, waiting for her to will it into use — even subconsciously.

It was all he had to give her, to thank her for the wondrous gift she had given him tonight. He burned with the taste and feel of her, wanted more with every fiber of his being. With a wrenching moan he bent his head to taste that part of her that was almost as secret and magical as her blood. It would have to be enough for now, until she was ready for the next step, and he would have to honor that.

* * * * *

She came to herself after what were surely long, long moments.

"Sugar girl, my sweet Aerin, the taste of you...oh *the taste*!" Violanti's voice murmured softly, but no longer at her ear. He moaned the words again, repeating them like a litany, and it took her a moment to realize he spoke them against the still quivering flesh of her pussy.

His tongue was lapping at her, drinking her in. His lips moved against her as he said the words yet again. "The taste, the taste, oh I am lost." He speared her with his tongue, his fingers gently parting her folds wide for his adoring mouth.

"Violanti," she moaned, her voice no more than a rough whisper—for it had been spent during her earlier shouting.

He moved up at the sound of her voice, covering her again. His fingertips, stained with what looked like blood—if she'd had a virgin membrane he had surely ruptured it with his fingers by now—stroked against her cheeks. "Aerin, Aerin, my darling," he whispered, pressing reverent kisses all over her face.

She felt her breasts taken in one of his hands, felt her nipple pinched and pulled upon with careful tenderness. And that swiftly, her passion was reawakened. Impossibly, she wanted him as desperately as she had but moments before her release.

But Violanti surprised her. Instead of taking all that she offered, instead of thrusting that great thick cock of his into her once more starving quim, as she would have desperately liked for him to do, he merely held her. Kissed her. Fondled her.

"Please," she begged, beyond all shame.

His eyes were gentle and warm, fuzzy with his own passion. "Not tonight. Rest now. I've been too demanding. Later...later we'll have more. Later, when you're stronger. When you've rested."

The ever-changing rainbow of his gaze trapped her and lulled her. Keeping her safe. Easing her towards sleep.

"I never knew touching could be so purely exquisite, Aerin. Tonight you've taught me so much more than I'd hoped to teach you. Thank you. Thank you so much," his voice faded out. Those words, so full of raw emotion, yet still unable to keep sleep from claiming her fully, fell silent on her deaf ears as she rested.

Before she knew it he was waking her, telling her softly, regretfully, that it was time for her to go.

Chapter Seven

"You look like you have a secret," Heather teased over their fast-food lunch.

Aerin smiled against her will, feeling the warmth of the previous evening wash over her with a gentle pleasure. "I was just thinking of the new clothes I bought," she lied. Her voice had risen to be heard over the din of the mall's bustling food court but was still a little raw from all the moans and shouts Violanti had wrung from her in the blue room's bed. "I can't imagine that I'll ever dare to wear them, even if they are gorgeous."

"That's precisely why you'll wear them," Heather affirmed with a laugh. "You look gorgeous in them. It would be a shame for you to bury them in the back of your closet behind all that drab and depressing business attire you seem to love wearing day in and day out."

"Are you trashing my clothes?" Aerin wriggled her eyebrows comically. She, too, hated her drab clothing, but she knew she was too fat and too ugly to wear the bright, stylish clothes that were so in fashion.

The styles of clothes that stuffed her shopping bags, for instance, were meant for people who looked like Heather. Svelte, attractive, and smart looking people wore clothes like those. Not egg-shaped ragamuffins like herself.

But when she'd tried the clothes on…she'd felt truly pretty. For the first time in, well, forever. She'd felt taller, slimmer, and prettier. It had been a decadent and wondrous feeling. The look in Heather's eyes had added to that, a look of appreciation and approval, and Aerin had felt certain she did look good. That it hadn't only been her wistful imagination tricking her.

She had bought the clothes.

But would she wear them? She didn't know. Maybe. Just maybe.

Perhaps for Violanti. If she decided to go back to Fetish and see him again. That was up for debate in her mind at this point. She did so want to see him again, to finish what had started between them, but she didn't want to blow so much money on the experience. No matter how wonderful an experience it might, and very probably would, be. She wasn't rich, after all, and the money in her savings wouldn't last her forever. For now she would have to think about it.

She would think about wearing the clothes, and about perhaps showing them off to Violanti if she should decide to return to Fetish once again.

Heather laughed. "Yes! I am trashing your clothes. You looked so good in those bright colors, I can't believe you'd even think of not wearing them. You're the kind of person who shines in bold and beautiful attire, but you just don't want to believe it."

"You are so full of it," how much fun it was to have a friend with whom she could tease and laugh, "I'm too fat to wear purple and scarlet. I only end up looking like a circus tent when I do."

"Well your diet is working wonders on your figure, so you won't have that excuse to hide behind much longer. As if you did in the first place. You're not fat at all. You're—"

"Big-boned? I've heard that one too many times," Aerin snorted. And what diet? She wasn't on any diet. Heather wasn't the first person to notice her weight loss either; there had been others, including herself. She was wearing smaller sizes recently, only a few digits down, but still, it was an improvement—one she'd quickly noticed. Perhaps menopause was helping to speed up her metabolism?

"I wasn't going to say *big-boned*," Heather laughed, "I was going to say that you're baroque. You know, plump and curvaceous and beautiful, like all those old paintings you see in museums."

"I know baroque and I love that period, but I am not like that. I'm pale and plain and fat. Not rosy or cute or rounded, like those old world hussies," she laughed.

"But you are. You're just too stubborn to see it."

"Can we talk about something else? Like your fiancé?" Heather's long time boyfriend had finally proposed Friday evening, and from the size of the diamond on her finger, he was a well-landed catch indeed. "Tell me more about him."

Heather's eyes glazed over, and a look of besotted love turned her normally attractive face even more so. It fairly glowed. "Dan is wonderful. You know, we've been dating since high-school, but this was still a surprise." She brandished her engagement ring with excited glee. "I didn't think he'd want to marry until he made partner in the firm. He's so serious about his career. I was content to wait. This was just such a surprise...I almost didn't know what to say when he asked!"

"Well I'm glad you said yes, you deserve total happiness. Dan is lucky to have you," Aerin toasted with her paper cup full of fizzling soda. "He seems smart enough to know that, too. Good boy."

"He *is* a good boy," Heather giggled. "Too good for me, but I'm glad he hasn't figured that out yet. I don't know what to expect these next few months. He wants the wedding to be in July. That's only three months away. And," her eyes shadowed abruptly, "he wants me to quit my job after the wedding."

Aerin felt her eyes widen. "That's a bit archaic of him isn't it? Or do you want to quit your job? I wouldn't really blame you if you did."

"You know, I kinda do," she sighed. "I don't think I'm cut out for the corporate world, you know? It seems too cutthroat for me. And I'm not exactly enamored with my job either. But that doesn't give Dan the right to push me into quitting."

"If you're unhappy with the job, why did you decide to try working for the company in the first place?"

Heather's face lit up again and she leaned closer across the small eatery table, as if she were about to impart some great secret and didn't want it overheard by any who might pass. "Well, I'm a fast typist. Really fast. I can crank out orders like it's nobody's business. It really seemed smart when I was in school, to make use of that skill and to profit from it somehow. It's just that I'm so fast because in my spare time I write novels. Practice makes perfect, you know? Lots and lots of practice. The more I write, the faster I get. So I work in a print factory for a steady paycheck, but it doesn't make me happy. It's writing that really gets me excited. But I couldn't make a living at that."

Heather was so animated, so passionate. Suddenly sure that Heather did belong in the world of the novelist,

Aerin nodded thoughtfully. "I bet you could make a living at it, if you really focused on it. Maybe that's why Dan is asking you to leave your day job. Does he know you like to write?"

"Of course. I tell him everything! He knows how important that is to me. Not that it changes anything."

"I don't know, maybe it changes everything. Maybe he wants to give you this chance to be an author in the only way he can." Was this really her speaking these words? Aerin had never understood people, relationships, or the motives that drove human behavior. But this scenario seemed plausible, so she pointed it out. "Maybe he knows that you'd be happier writing full time and wants to give you that opportunity."

Eyes bright, Heather gasped, "But why wouldn't he just come out and say that? He simply told me he thought I should quit my job when we're married—like it was beneath him to have his wife working or something—not that I should write full-time."

"Well, I don't know him, so I can't speak for him. But what else would you do but write? Sit at home all day? If Dan knows you as well as you say, then he knows you'd probably use your time at the keyboard, composing. Not keeping house or making babies."

They fell silent for a moment. "You know, Aerin, I think you're right. I was just too concerned about keeping my independence, about not being bossed around by Dan, that I didn't see it. I'll ask him tonight if that's what he planned. Oh! Wouldn't it be incredible if I could write full-time?" she giggled and clenched her hands in a show of great excitement.

Aerin laughed with her friend. "It sounds like Dan can afford to pay the bills while you follow your dream. I hope I'm right in thinking that's what he means to do."

"I think you are right, Aerin. I think you are. How could you see something so clearly that I couldn't? You're such a great friend, you really are."

Blushing, Aerin took a deep drag from her soda. "You'd have thought of it too in a day or so."

"Come on. I've had enough of this greasy garbage," Heather sneered down at their food. "Let's celebrate my engagement and go buy some shoes." The two rose, threw the remnants of their meals in the nearest rubbish bin, and went off in search of the perfect buy. Aerin had never had so much fun at the mall. It was great to have a friend.

* * * * *

The next evening, Aerin forgot his face.

After fighting all day against the inevitable forgetfulness that she suspected lay just on the edge of her mind, she lost the battle, and Violanti's features once more blurred into the deepest recesses of her faulty memory. It happened in the shower, as she regretfully cleansed the last faint traces of his scent from her body. Her mind seemed to wander from the present, seemed to drift away to places unknown, and when she came back to herself she had forgotten him.

Tears had never tasted so bitter on her tongue. Weeping had never been difficult for her, but now it seemed painful and punishing, and in no way did it offer her relief. How could she be so stupid? How could she be so careless? Did nothing hold value for her anymore but her own self-centered depression?

For hours she asked herself these and countless other similar questions. She berated herself, hated herself, and wanted nothing more than to scream her frustration into the deep and lonely silence of her house. But she didn't scream. She gritted her teeth and squared her shoulders, both figuratively and literally, determined to triumph over what she was sure must be some strange case of menopause induced amnesia.

To triumph, she must go back to Fetish. She must see Violanti again. To remember his face, his scent, his touch, she must go back. Damn the cost, both in money and in pride, she simply had to go back and see him again. But only this one last time, no more. She was no fool to think she could start any lasting relationship with a paid escort from some sex club.

Even if Violanti seemed as interested in her as she was in him.

Violanti was paid to find an interest in her. Whether he admitted to it or not, that was the truth of the matter. And she, stupid spinster that she was, must never forget it. Yes, she'd had the time of her life last night. Yes, her body had been, and still was, his for the taking. But she must, deep down, still have ultimate control of her heart.

She'd actually *forgotten* his face in as little as twenty-four hours. Perhaps it wasn't her heart at risk after all, but instead her sanity.

No matter. It was her heart that must, ultimately, concern her. She must never give it to this escort, this dangerously sexy Violanti, or else risk the greatest hurt she'd ever known. She may be a virgin—well, perhaps not technically after last night—and she may have never been in love, but that didn't mean she was unaware of the pain such a love could bring. Love was a double-edged sword, even in the most perfect of situations, and this was by no means a perfect situation.

The color of her money orchestrated the behavior of her mysterious escort. She must never, ever forget it; certainly not as quickly as she had forgotten his face. Even as she enjoyed their time together, sweet as it was, it was but a dream. A dream that would not, could not, last.

Did he have brown hair or black? And what color were his eyes? That seemed the most significant of all else she'd forgotten, beyond the shape of his face or lips or length of hair. It was his eyes she should remember forever, surely. The windows to his soul, so deep and so strange. But what color were they?

The force of her sobs surprised her. She felt as if her heart and mind had betrayed her in the worst way. In a most unforgivable way. How, oh how, could she have forgotten his face? The face of her lover, her first and probably last, should always remain in her memory, should it not? How could the visage of her greatest desire be gone from her so soon and so completely?

She loved him, or was very close to it. Warnings or denials would do her no good. Already she was that far gone.

Damn her for a fool.

The ticking of her mantle clock, keeping time with the spill of each of her tears, was her only company that long and lonely night. And no matter how hard she tried, she could not remember his face. His beloved face.

Chapter Eight

Madame Delilah kissed both her cheeks in greeting, before crushing her in a hug that seemed far too strong for such a delicate looking woman. "I'm so glad you came back, love. Violanti is waiting for you in the pink room."

Aerin frowned and almost reached to push up the rim of her sagging glasses before she remembered she was wearing her new contact lenses. She wondered if she'd ever be able give up that habit, she'd been doing it for so long it had become reflexive. "Where is that?"

"I'll take you."

"But I haven't paid yet. And you didn't get me to sign the receipt from last time."

The Madame waved an airy hand in dismissal, clearly unconcerned and hurried. "Don't worry about that, it'll be taken care of whenever. For now, come on, you've got a whole night ahead of you just waiting to get started."

Following the Madame through a maze of different rooms — how many rooms could this mansion have anyway? — Aerin felt a euphoric anticipation grip her. Tonight was the night, she was sure of it. Tonight, she would make love with him! With Violanti, the most virile and handsome man she'd ever clapped eyes on. It was so exciting she barely kept herself from running ahead and dragging Delilah along behind her. She might have actually done so if she'd known the way.

The pink door, which undoubtedly led to the pink room, loomed before them. It was a soothing color, but titillating all the same. It was the exact shade of pink that might stain a virgin's white sheets after lying with her first lover. It was the same color as a woman's softest flesh; her lips or nipples or vagina.

Aerin knew her own sex was this same color; earlier in the day she'd shaved all her pubic hair away for the occasion, wanting no barrier between her skin and his. She knew—not from any mirror, as she rarely looked in one—but from memory, that her nipples and lips were also this same color. This was the color of sex. This was the color of making love.

"Go on through, he's waiting for you."

She smiled at the Madame, who in turn smiled back encouragingly, and went through the door. Her heart pounded, her lips and tongue dried out. This was it. Tonight was the night. These last few steps would be her last as a virgin. After this she would be completely made over into a woman.

Her thoughts and expectations were solidified when she caught sight of him.

With paintbrush in hand, painting wild and energetic strokes onto a canvas before him, he stood in the middle of the room. Naked but for black, thigh high vinyl boots. Large silver buckles stood out in cold, stark relief on the dark and shiny material. The rest of his body, glistening in the coral light of the room like a bronzed sculpture, was completely bare but for the tiny silver nipple ring, the silver talon in his ear lobe, and—this was new—the silver stud that pierced the crown of his bobbing cock.

His fetish for silver shone like a beacon in the dim lighting. His eyes, too, were silver. More silver than green or blue tonight. His face was familiar once again, as handsome and dashing as ever. After her frightening week of trying desperately to remember how he looked and failing to do so, she was surprised he felt so familiar, as if her memory had never been locked against him. It must be the onset of menopause that was causing these memory quirks. She resolved to visit her doctor and add hormone therapy to her treatment, as soon as possible. That should fix things.

That wonderful smell that seemed to emanate from his very pores tickled her senses. She breathed deeply. The small noise seemed overly loud in the quiet of the room and Violanti's eyes met hers over the easel and canvas that stood between them.

"You're not wearing your glasses."

"I'm wearing contacts." She didn't need to tell him they were new, that she'd waited this long to buy a pair, and all because she'd wanted to see him clearly at all times. Especially when they had sex.

"I've a gift for you," he said simply, changing the subject.

She blushed, hearing the subtle innuendo in those words. His cock was swollen and at attention, quite obviously aroused at being so bared before her very approving gaze. "What is it?" Her voice felt thick in her throat. Arousal swamped her. That quickly, without even a touch or kiss shared between them, she was ready for him.

He smiled, clearly not unaware or unaffected by her open interest in his body. "Come. Look and see for yourself."

Again that double entendre, but she realized he only meant for her to look at the painting. She moved to stand close beside him so that his body heat warmed her, turned to view the canvas, and gasped.

It was a portrait of her, completely nude, facing forward with Violanti's body cushioning her back. His hand rested on her hip possessively. His hair fell forward to tangle with hers, his mouth played about the crook of her neck. Her eyes were closed, her face soft and lovely. Her lips were full and parted. Her breasts were round and smooth, her belly gently curved, her hips full and lush, but in no way did she look fat. Or plain. Or ugly. She looked lush.

How could this be? Was this person in the painting really her? She recognized it as her. But Aerin knew she couldn't look like this—this lovely, exquisite, *beautiful* woman—lying supine in the painting. She just couldn't. It was impossible.

"Not impossible," Violanti's words made her wonder if she'd spoken her thoughts aloud, or if he's just sensed them as he seemed so easily able to do, "for you are beautiful. You just don't see it in yourself. But you will. I'll show you how gorgeous you are." He leaned over and gave her temple a soft whisper of a kiss. He set his brush and pallet down and turned to her with a dangerous, seductive smile.

"You can't take this painting home tonight. It has to dry first. But I'll send it to you when it's ready. For you to remember me, to remember us together."

Did he know she had such a hard time recalling him and their time spent with each other while she was away? How could he? He was very knowing, very astute, but not psychic. She almost laughed at that fanciful thought.

His gaze roved over her, changing colors in their kaleidoscopic way. "You look stunning tonight, sweet."

She was wearing a dark red dress, in crushed velvet. The waist was high, the hem was short, the cut like a baby doll dress. After much internal debate she'd begun wearing her new clothes, though it had been Wednesday before she'd dared try. It had taken her a few days to screw up enough courage.

Violanti wasn't the first to notice and appreciate her new style of dressing, but his was the first opinion that truly mattered to her. The realization was a surprise, but she found it much to her liking. She was concerned less and less of late, with how people viewed her. For once in her life she was oblivious and unconcerned with her outward image. She liked her new look, Violanti obviously liked her new look, and that was all that mattered.

"Thank you," she blushed. No matter how confident she grew, and she *had* grown more and more confident over the past few weeks, she knew she would always blush too easily.

"Scarlet is a wonderful color for you. It brings out the auburn depths of your hair."

That only made her blush harder, of course. But his words were light and sweet, and he was looking at her dress not her cheeks. She'd never known she had auburn in her hair. It has always seemed a dull, drab brown to her. How lovely to think that there might be hidden rainbows of color in her hair, brought out by these new colors and fabrics she was finally daring to wear. "You look very handsome too," her heart pounded.

"I find I paint much better in the nude," one of his ebony eyebrows swept up, "and I thought perhaps you'd find you liked me this way tonight. Easily accessible and bared to your gaze," he dared her to deny it.

"I do," she wouldn't, *couldn't* lie to him, "I do like it—you—this way," she stuttered then laughed ruefully at her own awkwardness—something she would have been unable to do but a few weeks ago.

"Good. Now, much as I like your dress, I think it's past time you took it off. Don't you?" His teeth were so white when he smiled that satyr's smile.

"Already? Aren't you going to offer me some wine to loosen me up first? Maybe give a kiss of greeting or something to encourage me?"

A growl of laughter raced from him, touching her in places that were ready to be touched ever more deeply—by other things besides his sexy amusement. "Was my gift of the painting not enough," he teased. "You, my sugar girl, need no further encouraging. I think you've bloomed quite well into a daring minx on your own, without need of liquor or other similar niceties."

"All girls need niceties, don't they?" What kind of man used a word like niceties in this day and age anyway?

His gaze burned. "Yes. Perhaps you're right." Leaning down, slow and seductive, he brought their lips together. Her eyes fluttered shut. His were cool, but quickly warmed against hers as they burned with her rising passion. The long fingers of his hands moved to frame her face, to tilt it just so, to better accommodate his kiss.

The flame of his tongue licked out and flickered against her lips until she parted them. It delved for a quick taste into the recesses of her mouth, giving her a taste of cinnamon sweetness, and then retreated. His lips nibbled against hers for a brief second more and then the kiss was ended.

"I'm glad you came back, Aerin. I missed you. If I seem rushed tonight it's because of that," he whispered against her mouth.

Her eyes opened and locked with his. "I missed you too."

"I dreamed of you."

"You did?" She felt her eyes widen, felt her heart thud like a liquid fist in her chest.

The curve of his lips tickled her mouth. Barely a breath separated them. "I did. And in my dream I did all the things I wanted to do to you. You loved it. You loved me. We loved each other."

She shied away from such words, not wanting to hear the echo of them sound in her blood. Pulling away from him, she averted her gaze, desperate to put some distance between them and fast.

Violanti let the moment go, easing her somewhat by allowing her to retreat. Love, she was sure, had no place here between them. Only money. Only lust and passion and desire. Those things she could handle, or at least, she thought she could handle them better than love. That he was likely saying such sweet words because he felt she wanted to hear them made them all the more disturbing.

Love should not be spoken of so lightly. Even she, lonely middle-aged woman that she was, knew this truth.

"Tonight I think you are ready for a very important lesson in your journey."

Aerin smiled, easing further as that odd moment passed, though a dark desire beat at her mercilessly in reminder. "And what is that?"

"Sex. Fucking. Making the beast with two backs. And what those things can and cannot mean between a man and woman. Later I'll show you the very real, very big difference between fucking and lovemaking, but for tonight I think you're as ripe and ready as I for a much baser lesson."

She frowned, not liking the hard edge in Violanti's voice. Whereas the night had at first seemed headed in a more tender direction, here he was telling her that tenderness had no place in what they would do together. It was just as well, she realized in the back of her prudent mind, for she was paying for sex here. One had to earn the trust and tenderness that came with true lovemaking. No amount of money could buy those things.

His staring gaze befuddled her thinking, both thrilling and frightening in their intensity. "Look at me, Aerin. Tonight I will be a tool, strong and hard, that you must use to find fulfillment. You will learn that sex *is* all it's cracked up to be and more, and you'll learn to reach out and take it when it's offered. You'll learn to like it, to need it, to go out and get it."

"W-what about you? Will you like it too?"

"Oh yes, I'll like fucking you, sugar girl. I'll love it. I already need it, as you can see if you'll just look down."

She did and swallowed hard when she saw just how *much* he needed it. He hadn't seemed so big last time. So thick. But that was just her imagination playing tricks on her, overreacting now that she knew for certain this part of him would be thrusting into her before the night was done. It was a terrifying and awesome knowledge. It nearly brought her to her knees.

"You're scaring me, Violanti," she moaned, but in desire more than fear despite her words.

"No. I'm *thrilling* you. There's a difference," he said arrogantly. His gaze burned. "And you like it, don't you?"

She did. Oh how she did. "You won't hurt me."

Something close to shock widened his eyes before they shuttered, hiding that show of surprise as if it must be kept secret. "I would never hurt you, Aerin. You're safe with me. Safe enough."

Safety had nothing to do with it.

"But I will ride you, and ride you hard. Don't ask for mercy, for I will spare you none. Not tonight, my sugar girl."

"You'll make me like it." How calm she sounded, when she felt like screaming.

That wicked smile of his again. "Of course. I'll make you love it."

"You're a devil."

He laughed, this time it was a roar that filled the room and made her smile helplessly in response. "I *am* a devil. It's a good thing you've noticed and are at ease with it, for it is fact." His accent was thick and rich and tickled over her mind deliciously. "Now," he sobered abruptly, "take off your clothes."

The thud of her heart filled her throat. With unsteady hands she did as he instructed, removing her dress by pulling it over her head. Her hair, which was oddly longer and thicker now than it had been when first they'd met, fell low about her shoulders in tangled disarray. Her bra, a front clasp of wispy lace as new as the dress, was quickly thrown to the floor as well. Her high-heeled shoes, red to match the dress, she kicked off carelessly. But when her hands moved to the black lace thigh highs, he halted her.

"No. Let me." He bent down before her and slowly peeled the silk down to her ankles. To steady herself, she rested her hands on his shoulders. Those thick muscles made her fingers itch to knead them and she didn't even bother to fight against that urge. The feel was exquisite. She dug her nails lightly into the smooth, strong firmness and was gratified by his gasping response.

That ebony black head of his came back up, her stockings removed now—her last barrier gone—to level with her up-thrust breasts. With every breath she made they trembled. His eyes followed their slightest move with a hunger that terrified her. Excited her.

His fingers brushed over the exposed sensitivity of her mons. "Minx. You wear no panties. How mad that would have driven me, if I'd but known."

"I've only been here fifteen minutes. You could have suffered that," she teased in an unsteady, breathless voice.

"I'd have jumped you in the first five." His teeth nipped playfully at her nipple—they seemed so sharp!—before pressing his lips against the tightly puckered flesh. She gasped. "Now. Lie back upon the bed, love."

She'd been oblivious to the bed, the large cream and pink confection should have seemed feminine, but the dark wood of the large wooden frame gave it an almost dangerous look. All that masculine wood surrounding the feminine frills...like a man and woman making love...it was very sensual.

Her imagination was far too fanciful tonight. Perhaps it was the mixture of Violanti's scent and that of his paints that caused it. She didn't know or care.

Long-fingered hands guided her to the bed and eased her back upon the pillows. "We've been here before," she lightly offered, referring to their last encounter.

"Not like this," he countered. "And never like it again; you're innocent only once."

"I'm not so innocent anymore, thanks to you."

His smile was frightening, dark, and possessive. "Then all is as it should be."

He covered her breasts with his hands, lying down upon her easy and light, so as not to crush her with his weight. His skin seemed warmer than usual tonight against hers, but was as hard and firm as she remembered. Harder still as the hot ridge of his erection pressed into her belly.

The moist sweet flavor of his breath played over her lips. "I want you," his murmur was as unsteady as the pulse that beat through her blood, "badly."

It made her feel beautiful, the way he was looking at her, the way he was reacting to her. Sexy. And very vulnerable. She could find no words, and didn't need to, for he claimed her mouth with an electrifying intensity that bordered on aggression.

He moved down her body, kissing her cheek and jaw and neck. A dangerous sizzle of pleasure raced through her as she felt his teeth nibble her throat before moving down to claim her aching nipples. He sucked one into his mouth, tonguing it to a diamond hardness.

The strength of his body caged her, enfolded her. His hands bit into her sides as he moved to settle between her legs. The heat of his cock pressed into the aching cradle of her thighs, prodding at the folds of her pussy. She was wet and more than ready, or her body was. Her mind was a quagmire of pleasure and nervousness, fear and lust.

His hands tightened, nearly bruising her. Catching her to him with a barely suppressed show of violence, she saw and felt Violanti's mouth open impossibly wide to take the fullness of her breast deep into his mouth. Deep, searing pain shocked her as he bit deep. His teeth felt like needles, long and stabbing deep towards her heart.

Pleasure burst. Like a tsunami it washed over her, and she was powerless to fight against it. She raked her nails down his back, knew she drew blood, but didn't care. She couldn't stop. There was too much ecstasy. Too much exquisite pleasure. Her body screamed with it. Her mouth opened to let out that scream, as her body shuddered beneath his.

His hand came up to cover her mouth, to stifle the earth shattering sound. She felt it seal against her mouth even as another scream erupted. Her sex pounded, the walls of her pussy trembled and quaked, her hips bucked wildly against his.

Warm, liquid climax, centered in her pussy and in her breasts, washing back and forth all through her body until she was maddened by it. She shouted again and lost all sense of self.

Chapter Nine

The taste of her filled him. Her essence flooded through his every cell. The taste of her ecstasy was spicy and intoxicating and monumentally impossible to resist.

He swallowed the magical sweetness of her blood, feeding the thirst that drove him.

His soul bathed in the golden vortex of her blindingly bright aura, energized by the force that fed her life and sustained his.

He spread her legs, wishing briefly that he'd been more careful, more patient with her. That he'd given her more time to prepare for this, their first joining. But he could not. As was always true, she stripped him bare, left him bereft of any self-control, any reason. He wanted her. He had to have her. Nothing else mattered.

Rising up, he breathed over the punctures in her gorgeous, delectable breast. His breath would seal the wounds, help them heal and fade in but seconds. His sugar girl was shrieking softly into his hand, all but swooning with pleasure thanks to the magic web he wielded instinctively as he fed.

She was so beautiful.

He wanted more.

And more he would have. He positioned himself at the portal of her wet heat and waited for her to come back to the moment. When her eyes met his, he let his own open fully, let her see the red stain of his bloodlust, of his love, and impaled her in one long thrust.

* * * * *

She cried out, seeing the red haze of his eyes, like some demon's. They burned into her, invading her very soul, and then he filled her with his body.

Her cry changed to a scream, but not of pain. There was no pain. Only passion. And the fear caused by his red eyes blended with that passion until there was only hot, naked lust.

The thick, long length of him stretched her body tight. Like a new glove her sheath struggled to accommodate his girth and succeeded. Barely. Aerin felt split wide open by him. Her cunt burned and throbbed, but the moment he stilled — imbedded at last to the hilt — all discomfort faded away, replaced by pleasure. Only pleasure.

"God," she squeezed her eyes shut against the wondrous ease, and the frightening impossibility of his crimson gaze. "Oh god."

His weight was held supported on his hands, rising high above her so that his muscles bulged. The thick flesh of him jerked within the depths of her body and they both moaned. "So wet, so tight," he groaned. "*Fuck.*"

A bead of sweat fell from his face to splash onto her cheek. It fairly sizzled on her feverish skin.

"Wrap your legs around my waist," he demanded.

He was so deep, so thick, and she couldn't find the strength to move.

"Hurry." He moved, a rocking motion of his hips, as if he couldn't help himself.

She wrapped her legs around him, locking her ankles in the dip of his back to hold them fast. Unbelievably, his body sank even deeper into her. Aerin shrieked and bucked reflexively against the blinding pleasure this new angle brought. Her clit was mashed against him, their bodies flush and tightly joined, and deep within she felt a new sensation where that wicked silver bar in his penis caressed her.

"I can't...can't wait..." His body trembled against her, shaking her body along with his, shaking the bed. And then he moved. And moved. And moved. He thrust hard, going deeper, then withdrew. His hips arched then came slamming back down into her, filling her with the thick, hot swell of his hard skin.

The strength of his hands seemed incredible as they moved to guide her, to teach her the movements that would bring her the most pleasure. He lifted her full weight off the bed, to move her on his cock as easily as he might have moved his hand. His strength frightened, but thrilled her, for part of that preternatural power helped to drive his thrusts hard and deep into the heart of her.

Her very bones hummed and vibrated.

The full weight of her breasts shook with the force. Violanti leaned back, bringing her with him so that he sat back on his heels. She straddled him now. He guided her every movement upon his glistening, bronzed body with his hands under her buttocks. Their bodies slapped together. He grunted and bucked his hips as he brought her down with a particularly strong bounce.

Aerin cried out, digging her nails into his shoulders as she sought solid purchase in the storm of their passion.

"Come for me, sugar girl. Let me feel that honey pussy squeeze and squeeze *and squeeze*," he panted against her mouth.

His fingers dug into the cushion of her ass, bringing her tight against him, then lifting her up for another thrust. Her clit swelled and throbbed. Her pussy stretched and flooded over his deeply impaling cock.

The full, firm grimace of his mouth moved to the curve of her neck and shoulder. "Come on love. Give it to me," he urged, breath harsh beneath her ear. His tongue licked out.

Her clit brushed against him. Her legs tightened. He thrust deep again, filling her, taking all of her in one deep move. Her cunt throbbed, pulsed. Heat rose in her womb, swamping her. Pleasure sang from head to toe, until her scalp ached. Another deep thrust, another pulse, and she flew straight into the heavens.

"That's it baby, come for me. Milk me. Swallow me up." His mouth opened over her and there came again that deep stab of teeth. Warmth flowed from her to him. Her body jerked on his. His hands came up to clutch at her back, catching her tightly against him.

His hips bucked between her legs. Filling and stretching her, his thrusts growing harder and faster. His head whipped back as he shouted, a deafening ululation, and warm liquid splashed on her throat and breasts. It stained his mouth.

She screamed, in fear and in pleasure, still climaxing. Hot, scalding warmth burned her womb and she screamed again. Pleasure and pain, pain and pleasure—she was driven mad by it. And it didn't matter. Nothing mattered but this wondrous, amazing man in her arms. The image of his bloodstained mouth faded, her mind turned away from it, and all fear of him fled.

Violanti thrust one last, powerful time into the heart of her. They both cried out and trembled like two leaves in a hurricane wind. They clutched tightly at each other, wanting no separation, needing to be as close as possible in that moment.

Minutes passed. They collapsed back onto the bed, limp. Their breaths calmed, but only just. Violanti licked her clean from neck to nipple, each pass of his tongue ringing another milking tremor from her pussy. The hard length of him still filled her, as hard as ever, stretching her. The thick mixture of his come and hers trickled teasingly down the crease of her ass.

The room seemed unnaturally hot. Violanti rolled, taking her with him, his body still joined to hers. She rested atop him now, shaken and spent. The thunder of his heart lulled her. The deep, steady drag of his breath into his lungs was timed perfectly with hers.

An explosion of sound as the door flew open startled a soft cry out of her. Violanti moved immediately to shield her from the unexpected, uninvited intruder.

"Come quickly! There's been an accident." The man was another escort at the club, and quite obviously shaken.

Violanti's body was a blur of motion as he rose. He moved quickly to join the man at the door. Unconscious or uncaring of his nudity, he wasted no time to dress, yet he still sported his wicked black boots. He paused only to spare her one level stare before he left. "Stay here," he commanded imperiously. Without his seeming to touch it, the door shut firmly closed behind him. The lock clicked the minute the latch caught, sounding like a gunshot in the room.

Panicked, shocked and confused, Aerin trembled, pulling the bedclothes protectively around her. *What the hell is going on?*

She hadn't the faintest idea.

Chapter Ten

Violanti looked at the cold, lifeless, human body slumped across the bed. One other occupied the room; a male vamp newly arrived to the club but two years ago. Two years was a very short time to their kind, so long as willing sex or blood could be found, but it had been a long enough time for the young Mitchell to cause trouble. Well, Mitchell was dead now, but that held no satisfaction for Violanti, who would have to clean up the mess he'd left behind. "*Maledire.* Damn him!"

"How could this have happened? In this house?" Delilah gritted out, livid with her own anger at the situation. She had arrived at the scene before Violanti by mere seconds, long enough to realize what had happened, but not long enough to think of a solution to the problem they now faced. *"With one of our own?"*

"He was *not* one of our own. Mitchell is — was — newly made. And no one here made him; he came to us from a coven in Chicago. We took him in because of a favor owed to that family. Don't you remember?" Robin, the one who had immediately gone in search of Violanti after discovering the horror of the two dead men, offered the explanation in a weak and worried tone, knowing it mattered little in the face of this tragedy.

Violanti's hard gaze chilled him to his toes. "Then that family owes *us* now, and plenty, does it not? To release a fledgling, one so obviously careless and inexperienced, into our midst is tantamount to sabotage. Our secrecy is at stake, and our secrecy is what keeps us alive. All of us. Damn him," he shouted once more, impotent with rage, "the *fool*."

"Burn Mitchell's body to ash. Do it now before I tear his heart out and eat it!" Robin moved immediately to obey the Madame's command. Lifting Mitchell's limp weight in his arms as easily as he might have lifted a sack of feathers, he turned to leave the room. The incinerator, in the dungeon basement of the mansion, would destroy all traces of the careless vampire.

But the human's body could not be disposed of so easily. Not so long as their coven's honor was to be upheld, in any case.

"What shall we do? This has never happened—"

"Find out who he is. Who might be looking for him and if they will ask too many unwanted questions," Violanti instructed in a terse, matter of fact tone.

Delilah thought for a moment. "I already have your answers. He's been a regular here, has been coming for almost a year, and he was almost exclusively Mitchell's lover. He has no close ties to family or friends. Those who might look for him won't find it too hard to ignore niggling suspicions if offered enough money."

"If you are right then we are very lucky indeed. Clean him. Then see to the proper placement of his body and effects."

"How could this have happened," she murmured again, looking close to shell-shocked now, rather than enraged.

"Mitchell was young. He did not understand the consequences of his actions, or just how great his responsibility was to his human lover. He fed too much and followed his prey into death. If his birth-coven would have seen to his education properly this need not have happened."

"What shall we do with them?"

Violanti knew the Madame meant the coven in Chicago, not the two dead lovers. "They will be offered the opportunity to make amends. If they do not appease us then we will destroy them utterly."

"They will fear us if I but mention our coven master's name." Delilah's smile was twisted over the deadly glint of her now erect fangs. "I know they will beg for the chance to redeem their gross mistake."

"Is my name so feared among our kind then?"

"You know it is."

"Then tell them my name. Tell them the Coven of Violent Dark has been offended. Tell them I will have their swift and ample apology or their hearts on a platter, I care not which."

Delilah bowed to him, hearing the power of his command, rightfully his as head of their 'family'. "It will be as you say."

"Good." He turned away, not wanting to see the proof of what he now thought of as his own failure to monitor the untutored actions of one of his own. He made his way back to his rooms, brooding.

For close to twenty years now he'd been watching over Fetish. The club had initially been his idea, a way for his people to live comfortably in the now smaller world of the new millennium. He had taken twenty of his friends and twenty of their friends to people his new-age coven, and until tonight everything had been close to perfect. His kind needed sex, needed blood, as humans needed food to live. But unlike humans, his kind had to coax their prey to willingness. Neither blood nor sex could be shared between their races without a human's consent—subconsciously or consciously, it mattered not which—but it had to be absolute.

If either blood or pleasure were taken by force or if too much blood was taken without being swiftly returned, death was most often the result, for both the vampire and human. As it had been for Mitchell and his human friend.

Stupid fledgling! Violanti felt the heat of his anger and nearly roared with it. But he wasn't only angry with Mitchell. He was angry with himself as well. As coven master, he should have seen this coming. But he'd been too busy sliding skin to skin with prey of his own, to worry about the safety of another.

The scent of Aerin filled his nostrils. The touch and taste and sound of her swamped his senses until he nearly reeled. Would the mere remembrance of her body beneath his always affect him so? He felt weak and strong, starving and completely satiated, all at once. His mind and heart were at war, as they'd never been with any other lover—human or otherwise—and it alarmed him on an elemental level he'd never even known he possessed.

Was he unwise to bond with her so? To share his fluid, any fluid, with her was close enough to a pair bond that if any of his people caught wind of it they would already consider her his blood-wife. Perhaps he should have used a condom.

But even the thinnest layer of latex could not have protected her if, in the heat of the moment, he'd not wanted it to. And he hadn't wanted that barrier between them, no matter how insignificant, not even for a moment. He'd wanted to feel her. Wanted to feel the hot, naked, honeyed walls of her clamping down on him as she came in a flood beneath him. She'd been liquid sunlight in his arms.

It was the closest he had been to the sun in over five hundred years.

If anyone had passed him in the passageway they would have seen his enormous erection. But no one was there. He would have ejaculated if not for his monumental control. Control that had weakened where the unfortunate Mitchell was concerned. A pity that. A shame he had to bear. But the Chicago coven would pay, Delilah would see to that. And the human's body would be taken care of, along with whatever family or friends he might have left behind. It was a tragedy, what had happened beneath his roof tonight, but their kind risked such horrors every night of their existence.

He only wished he could expunge the horrible guilt he felt over it all.

The storm of his thoughts and emotions confused him. He was never like this. Cool, calculating, and dangerously methodical, these things were what made him so formidable among his own kind. Not this possessive hunger, this restless desire, or this dark and terrible guilt that intertwined into one mass of puzzling disquiet.

Aerin weakened him.

But she also made him stronger than he'd ever felt before.

Should he bespell her, make her forget him and her time here so that they might both go their separate ways? He growled with angry loss at the very idea. But could he continue with her as he was, seeing her only once every week? Feeling her, smelling her, tasting her but once every seven long and lonely days? He knew that he could not. Not after tonight. After he'd been buried so deep inside of her that he felt the loss of her even now like a bleeding wound in his soul, after only a mere hour of separation.

He was losing his rigid control, over himself and his coven. Fetish could not afford another mistake like the one that had happened tonight. Something would have to change. And quickly. For the first time since he'd been made into what he now was, he felt the pressure of time weighing on him like a taunting specter, at last finally given leave to punish him for his long, ageless years.

He heaved a sigh outside of the pink room, where his human consort awaited him. Palming his tumescence in a rough hand, he let his worries fade for the time being. Aerin could not know of his troubled thoughts and heart. He would not ruin her time with him by burdening her with negativity. She had enough of that in her life outside these walls and he would not add to it.

Besides, he needed all of his energy focused on keeping her unaware of his true nature. Already she suspected, though she was afraid to confront those fears. She'd seen his lapses, his red eyes and bloodied mouth, but she'd turned away from them like a waking child from a bad nightmare. She wasn't ready to know what he was. Or what he had in store for her.

And just what *did* he have in store for her?

He'd be damned if he knew the answer to that question himself.

* * * * *

Aerin stared at the soft pink hue of her surroundings. Her throat was sore, her neck felt bruised and swollen. She knew why...but refused to accept it. There was a limit to how much she could accept just now, and *that* was beyond the pale. For now, she was focused more on the new sensations of her well-loved body than on frightening hysterical imaginings brought on by hormones during the most incredible orgasm — *multiple* orgasm — she'd ever had.

And just what had that fuss about an accident been all about? Violanti had been gone nearly an hour and she'd been trapped here, locked in until he came back to let her out. Was everything okay? Had anyone been hurt — was it that kind of accident? And why should Violanti care, shouldn't Madame Delilah be the one seeing to it instead of him? Or had it directly involved him in some way, whatever *it* was?

An ache throbbed in her womb and a warm trickle of her and Violanti's mingled fluids fell from her pussy onto the bed. That fluid was stained a rosy pink, like the room, either from the breaking of her hymen or...something else. She pulled the covers tight to her chest and winced at the raw tenderness between her legs. Her cunt felt swollen and empty, as if it had been stretched for Violanti, and now that he was gone it was bereft, longing for his return.

Her heart felt much the same.

Confusion bombarded her. Her mind and body were a storm of turbulent emotions she'd never felt before. Emotions she didn't understand. She'd just had sex with a man who was paid for such a thing. And she'd felt no guilt. No shame. Only pure and amazing pleasure.

Was that a bad thing? Did that make her a bad person? She didn't feel that it was so, but general society would undoubtedly find nothing but contempt for what she'd done here in Violanti's arms tonight.

What the hell do I care? I don't. So I paid a man to fuck me — it was wonderful and I'd do it again in a heartbeat. She smiled at herself, no longer surprised that her inner voice was getting a smart-assed attitude, as she had outwardly developed one more often than not lately. In fact, she reveled in the knowledge. She was getting stronger. The meek and mild Aerin of old was almost completely gone now. It was unbelievable, miraculous even, but it was nonetheless true.

She had Fetish to thank for that. *No.* She had Violanti D'Arco to thank for that.

Her clit burned and throbbed. She wished he'd come back. Her body already hungered for more of his touch. Her heart swelled with anticipation and — dare she even think it — love. Aerin had heard the saying that a woman would always love her first, and she thought now that might be true. Doubly so in her case. And what better man to love than Violanti? He was kind and considerate and smart and sexy as hell. Dangerous too. Deadly. She shivered, growing more and more excited, more and more eager for his return.

Plainly she was in lust with him already. And she was quickly falling in love with him. Heaven help her.

She wondered if heaven had anything even remotely to do with it.

The lock of the door clicked, like a firecracker going off in the silence. The door opened and Aerin jerked upright in the disheveled bed, her gaze flying to meet Violanti's eyes as he entered the room.

Eyes that were red as the dawn.

Chapter Eleven

"I want you on your knees, Aerin," he gestured before him, intentions clear.

She started at the unexpected command. "What happened? He said there'd been an accident, what—"

His gaze burned, filling her with alarm and confusion. How could his eyes be red? She shied away, mentally and physically. She didn't want to know that answer.

"On your knees. Now."

Unexpected anger heated her cheeks and breasts. He sounded so—so *hard*. So frightening. "I beg your pardon?"

A flash of teeth. "You heard me. Don't make me repeat myself a third time."

Angry, curious at this lightning quick change of his mood, and perhaps a little intimidated by it, she moved to stand before him. "You won't hurt me."

He growled, grabbed a fistful of hair at the back of her head and forced her to her knees before him. Shocked, she could only comply, and his strength was such that even if she'd thought to resist he would have overpowered her anyway.

The tip of his cock piercing glinted directly in front of her face. His hand held her head fast, tight, making her look at him as he towered over her. "Wet your lips."

"I don't think—"

"Do it."

"Violanti, you're scaring—"

He jerked her head up, bent down, and licked her lips himself. Her heart thundered. Her body was heavily aroused despite her alarm, her nipples hard and tingling, her pussy already hot and wet with need.

"Open your mouth. Wide."

She thought to resist, but the roaring flood of her own arousal drowned out any protests she might have made. And she felt sure that Violanti, this raging and volatile Violanti, would have ignored them anyway. She opened her mouth. As wide as she could.

"Now fuck me with your mouth, sugar girl," he commanded crudely.

She was compelled to pause, pucker her lips, and kiss him first. Her own overpowering desire and curiosity softened the moment despite his harsh and imperious insistences. His skin was hot and smooth as satin. He smelled so strongly here of almond and cinnamon that she felt nearly suffocated by it. Every breath she took was warm and thick with his delicious scent. She was dizzy with it.

The silver bar clicked against her teeth as she widened her mouth over him. He was so thick she had no chance of taking much between her lips, but she managed enough to swallow the crown into the back of her throat. Violanti's hand spasmed in her hair and was joined by the second as he guided her head over him. Glancing upward she could just see the thick muscles of his arms and chest as they bulged and trembled, and the sight of that gave her a feeling of immense power.

That she could weaken a man as strong as Violanti was exhilarating knowledge indeed.

Her lips stretched tighter over him. She moved over him, thrusting him in and out of her mouth as she suckled and licked every inch of him she could reach. He tasted like sweet, sugary almonds, as if he bathed in them. Wet, slurping sounds excited them both as her mouth moved over him again and again. Aerin had never thought that such primal, naked sounds could enflame her so, but they did.

The thick round head of him bumped the back of her throat and he shouted, hands mashing her face tighter against him until she nearly swallowed him. "Yes," his breath hissed out between clenched teeth, "just like that. Oh you make me want to *fuck*, sugar girl. I've been hard as a rock since the first moment I heard your voice."

The tender, considerate lover she'd grown accustomed to was no more. In its place was this amazing, earthy, demanding man and it excited her to no end. Her heart thundered, her blood roared. Every groan, every grunt he made as she sucked and licked him filled her with ecstasy.

"Suck me, yes just like that. *Maledire*. Your mouth feels almost as good as your pussy." He undulated his hips against her, thrusting his cock so deep in her mouth she saw stars.

The taste of him drowned her. The scent of him flooded her senses, made her crazy for him. No man had the right to smell so good. No woman on earth could have smelled him and not thought of crawling all over him. And Aerin vowed to herself that no woman would ever get the chance to taste him, not like this, not ever again. No woman, save her.

His hands cupped the sides of her head, stilling her, urging her to look up at him. She did. His eyes were silver again, then green, then blue and unbelievably, violet.

"I'm going to come in your mouth."

She shivered at the dark promise, wishing he'd get on with it, she was thirsting for it, starving for it. The heat in his gaze scorched her. His cock was still deep in her mouth, her lips swollen around it. She licked him and his hands shook against her face.

"You will swallow every drop. Won't you?" He sounded almost as if he needed her consent. "Every damn drop."

In assent, she slowly nodded over him and was wickedly delighted when his eyes swooned up in the back of his head. Her hands came up and cupped his balls, reveling in the cry she wrought from between his gritting teeth.

He moved then, creating a steady rhythm that she had no choice but to follow. His hands tangled in her hair again, clenching there spasmodically with every motion she made over him.

The thick weight of him was so hot in her mouth, so smooth and hard. She loved it, wanted more, took more until she might have gagged. He tasted so incredibly *good*.

"*Fottere mi,*" he whispered dreamily. "Fuck me, yes do it. Like that. Just a...little...more..." A pulse rippled through the length of him as she pulled and sucked. Hot, wet sweetness flooded her mouth and washed down the back of her throat. Violanti shouted, long and loud, until his roar of completion echoed off the walls around them. The taste of him, honeyed cinnamon, was delicious, and she eagerly swallowed every burst that erupted forth.

Burning, aching, yearning hunger overtook her. Her veins were on fire, thirsting for something she couldn't name or understand. With an eager need she feasted on him, on his ejaculate, as if it were some exotic candy that she could never have enough of. Her body shook. Strange, primitive noises escaped the back of her throat, vibrating along the length of him so that he swayed against her, spurting even harder into the depths of her hungry mouth. Sucking him, pumping him with her hands and mouth, she dredged up every bit of his essence and demanded more.

And still it was not enough.

Violanti let out a cry that was close to a scream, like some maddened jungle animal in the throes of passion, or pain, or a mixture of both. The last flood of him in her mouth was a trickle of sweetness compared to the storm of the first eruptions, and she lapped it up until nothing was left. Not one drop.

Limp and heavy, completely spent, Violanti collapsed back onto the floor, landing hard.

Crazed with lust, with frightening hungers she had no name for, Aerin crawled over him, mouth seeking. But he held her back, his strength diminished but still far too powerful for her to resist. Instead, he pulled her up his body, urging her to partake of a different sort of feast altogether.

Aerin straddled him. His cock was still hard as marble. Wet and shiny from her mouth, it stabbed up towards her so that she easily moved to impale herself on its thick length. Short, gasping screams erupted from between her swollen lips and she was powerless to hold them back as she sank down upon him.

So big. He was so big. She couldn't possibly take him in this position.

But she did. He filled her so fully, so deeply, she could have sworn that she felt him in the back of her throat.

"Give to me, Aerin. Give all of yourself to me."

She did. With his hands firmly grasping her hips to guide her, she began to ride him. Sinking up and down on his scorching hot cock, feeling it stretch her near to bursting, she rode him. Her nails dug into his shoulder as she clutched for purchase, for any anchor in this violence of passion and lust. Violanti growled, clearly enjoying the pain of her claws in his flesh, and thrust up into her. Thrust deep and hard enough to bruise.

Aerin screamed.

Violanti echoed her cry.

He pulled her down over him, taking one of her swaying nipples into his mouth hungrily. The long, lean strength of his fingers dug into the flesh of her ass, pulling and lifting her upon him in a rough gallop. His hips bucked into her down strokes, his mouth drew upon her nipple until it hurt. That sweet pain made her gasp. She ground her clit into him, rubbing hard against him, bouncing faster and faster on him with the help of his incredible strength.

Warmth spread in her chest. Her heart raced. Her head grew dizzy and faint. Her short, sobbing screams grew longer until they became wails. Her fingernails drew blood on his shoulders and chest, and Violanti thrashed beneath her.

A hot, liquid pulse like a fist or heartbeat, pounded deep inside her womb. It washed to every cell in her body, swamping her, taking her down, down into the ruthless shadows of pain and pleasure and ecstasy. "Violanti," she cried out his name over and over again. His mouth moved from her nipple to her mouth, drinking down her cries like drops of blood.

His hips crashed into hers one last time and, impossibly, she felt the splash of his come in her pussy as he found another release. For a moment she mourned the loss — she would so have liked to swallow him again — but if her mouth couldn't drink him down then at least her womb would. As if in echo to her thoughts, the walls of her cunt milked him, swallowing his liquid fire hungrily. Squeezing him, clenching him, making her shake and sob.

When she had calmed, she was laying full length upon him, limp and heavy. They were still joined, both wet and raw from their passion. The tips of his fingers were rubbing gently over the moue of her anus, each caress wringing another tremor from her already exhausted body.

Lying there, his fingers playing over her, her face buried in the crook of his neck, she smiled. And burst into joyous tears.

* * * * *

"It's almost dawn, love," he whispered.

They must have been lying on the floor like this for a long time. "How do you know," she murmured lethargically, not really caring how, merely wanting to prolong the moment.

"I can feel it."

That sounded like a leading statement, as if he wanted her to ask *how* he could feel it. How it was possible. But she didn't ask. Didn't want to ask. "Do I have to go then?" *Please say no.*

"Yes," he sounded weary now, maybe even a little disappointed. In her or in their situation? She didn't know.

He sat up with her easily. Too easily. She was astonished at how strong he was. Without even grunting over the burden of her weight he rose from their prone position, lifting her with him in a fluid motion that made her head swim. She giggled and burrowed her face deeper into the crook of his neck.

"Get dressed," he said gently, lowering her to her feet slowly, reluctantly. "Hurry."

She bent over to get her panties from the floor and immediately felt Violanti press his hardness into her. "Damn. Stand still." His hand shook as he put one hand on her back to keep her bent and filled her with one hard shove that slid in deep and wet and scorching hot.

Aerin cried out. Violanti thrust three times, deep hard thrusts that made her burn, then pulled out of her as swiftly as he'd filled her.

He bent down behind her and, shocking her to the core, he put his open mouth on her. The hot wet velvet of his tongue bathed her, stabbed deep, then laved away all her tenderness with erotic caresses.

"Omigod," she moaned.

His mouth moved up and he licked her anus, while one long finger thrust easily into her pussy. Quick as a snake, he rose up behind her again and pushed her from him, licking his lips as she turned to face him. She was dumbfounded.

"Why are you stopping — ?"

"You must get dressed. It's dawn and I can't...please get dressed, sugar girl. You drive me crazy with lust when you stand there naked and dazed. Come. I'll help you," and he moved to do just that.

Aerin was getting angry. How could he arouse her like that and just pull away. He was clearly in need of her, his body couldn't possibly hide that fact. So why not finish it? With an angry huff of breath she finished gathering her things and he led her to the door with a hand in the small of her back.

Unbelievably she didn't think he was even going to say goodbye to her. But as she stepped through the door he stopped her with a kiss on her pouting mouth. "You have no idea how wonderful you were tonight, Aerin. No idea how much I needed what you gave me. I hope you'll come back next Saturday night?"

Some wicked urge awakened inside her. The urge to hurt him as she was hurting over his abrupt dismissal. It was petty and it was rude and it was totally unlike her. And that was why she did it. "I'm not sure. I've got plans for next Saturday. Besides I can't really afford another trip to this place," she wouldn't have believed herself capable of it, but she managed a totally convincing flippant laugh after that bald-faced lie.

Violanti's eyes immediately flamed red. Her heart nearly stopped in her chest. What did it mean, that his eyes were so alien and so chameleon like? He didn't look human. In fact, he looked downright dangerous and deadly with his eyes like that.

"But you haven't been charged for coming here. Not since your first visit."

Aerin started. Surprised. "What do you mean? Of course I have. Madame Delilah—"

"She has waived your fees on my request. But for your initial visit here you haven't been charged a dime."

How surprising. She would check her bank account first thing Monday to see if he spoke the truth. Why would the Madame do that for Violanti? Were they close friends, was it a favor to him? She didn't understand.

"Break your plans, whatever they are."

Anger again. She was a bundle of emotions tonight, confusing, but liberating all the same. "No."

"Yes."

Why was she even arguing? She knew she'd be back here. He had to know it too. But she couldn't stop. "Don't tell me what to do, Violanti. I pay you remember? If anyone has the right to be bossy, it should be me."

His eyes widened, anger tightened the lines of his mouth. "You do not pay me. And I am bigger, stronger, faster, and older than you. That makes me the boss—"

Aerin laughed harshly, enjoying and hating their argument all at once. "Honey, you are not older than me. Not even close," though it flattered her that he might believe so. Even if it was an absurd belief. Anyone who looked at them together would know she was a lot older than he, surely. And for some reason this made her feel stronger, perhaps even a little superior to him.

He took that from her in an instant. "You're an infant as far as experience is concerned. I've lived more in my years, far more, than you."

"I'm leaving," she glared at him.

"You'll come back Saturday." It wasn't a question.

"I'll think about it," she surrendered tremulously. "Goodbye, Violanti."

He slammed the door behind her, anger vibrating in the horribly loud sound it made.

She couldn't get to her car fast enough. Peeling rubber as she pulled out of the drive, she wondered what the hell she'd gotten herself into with a man like Violanti.

That is…if he was even a man at all.

She had her doubts about that. A lot of them.

Chapter Twelve

The painting arrived Wednesday night, almost two full days after she'd somehow — once again — managed to forget Violanti's face. A teenaged boy, not much taller than her and skinny as a beanpole, brought the brown wrapped package to her door. Thinking the ringing of her doorbell signaled the arrival of Heather — they were going shopping again, Aerin's clothes were getting too baggy to wear — she didn't even check through the peephole before throwing wide the door.

"Ms. Peters?"

"Yes."

The young man held out his large parcel. "This is for you."

She started, reaching for it with a puzzled frown. Had she ordered something online and forgotten about it? She couldn't, for the life of her, remember. "Who's it from, do you know?"

"I dunno. My dad just framed it — he owns a shop on Third and Main — and said the guy who paid for it paid extra for us to deliver it by hand as soon as it was finished."

"Okay. Thank you." She reached for her purse, on a table by the door and pulled out five dollars. She offered him the tip and was surprised when he shook his head, grinning.

"That's okay. My dad would kill me if I took a tip, especially where such a wealthy client is concerned. He'd say it was 'bad business'," he laughed, obviously finding his old man's business philosophy a bit antiquated.

"Oh. All right. Thanks again."

"No problem. Later." He jogged off into the night, climbed onto a moped parked on the curb before her house and drove off with a jaunty wave.

Aerin closed the door and tore excitedly into the paper. Inside, was a beautiful painting done mainly in rich hues of shadowy crimson, gold, and black. The piercing silver stare of Violanti's gaze looked out at her from the portrait, as he lounged over and behind a dreamy rendering of her ripe nude body.

Like a tidal wave that made her sway weakly, she remembered everything.

Violanti's face and body, so beautiful it made her heart ache. As dark as a fallen angel—Lucifer in his prime had never been so endowed as her enigmatic, Italian lover.

His eyes…no *human* could have eyes like his. She shuddered, and the cold, metallic taste of fear washed through her mouth. They'd been red in the moments of his release. Crimson. The color of fresh, wet blood.

"How could I have forgotten?" And that was it, the million-dollar question, which held the key to everything that puzzled her about Fetish. About Violanti. About herself.

And she knew the answer, or at least some of it. It had nothing to do with menopause—she'd been to her doctor Monday just to be sure, and everything had appeared fine—and everything to do with *him*. With Violanti D'Arco, the strangest, sexiest man she'd ever met. She was as certain of that as she was of her own name. Her memory losses had started after she met him, after her first trip to Fetish, and she only forgot things that had direct links to the club and to her enigmatic lover.

Lover. The very word made her knees feel like water—it was that decadent. She still couldn't believe that she, mousy Aerin Peters, had actually taken a lover. But then, she wasn't so mousy, not anymore.

This was another change she attributed to Violanti, among others.

She'd lost weight—a lot of it—without even really noticing. It had been Heather who had finally pointed out how ill-fitting her new clothes were, and only just that day during their shared lunch break. Aerin hadn't changed her diet, hadn't exercised—she hated exercise—she hadn't done anything to facilitate her dramatic weight loss. Aerin had been confused, puzzling all day long about how she could manage to drop the pounds so easily after spending years yo-yo dieting with little or no results. But now that the risqué and downright arousing portrait was here in front of her, she knew that it had something to do with Violanti.

Clearer-minded now than she could ever remember being, especially in the past month, she gently propped the painting up against the cushions of her oversized sofa and went in search of the full length mirror in her guest bedroom.

With a flick of a switch, bright glaring light filled the room. The mirror was nearly hidden under a messy drape of sweaters and slacks—she rarely used it, and when she did it was to try on and discard clothing before going to work. Removing the rumpled clothing, she looked, truly looked, at herself in the harsh light of the room and was stunned. The sight of her reflection made her gasp and draw closer to the looking glass in disbelief.

How much she had changed! It was incredible that she hadn't noticed just how much before now. The transformation was incredible, miraculous. *Impossible.* More than one person over the past few weeks had remarked on her hair or her clothes or her weight loss, but it was amazing that they hadn't pointed these things out with a bit of well-warranted incredulity. She hardly looked like herself at all.

No longer was she overweight, limp-haired, and timid looking. Far, far from it, in fact. She looked healthy. Big-boned, she would always be big-boned, but trim and firm—a far cry from plump. Her legs looked long and shapely.

Her shoulders no longer looked so hunched in on themselves, but were strong and proud. She was standing straighter. She never stood straight, she was too unsure of herself. But here she was, looking like some noble Amazon, without even trying for the effect.

Her skin was translucent, with a rosy glow that enhanced her cheekbones, and the new concavity of her cheeks themselves. Her face was leaner, free of any blemishes, smooth and soft. Her jaw line was square—square for goodness sake—when it had been almost round the last time she'd really looked at it, and her chin looked almost stubborn beneath the soft curve of her mouth.

The locks of her hair were shinier, impossibly longer, and thicker. There was more body to her hair, more color. The usual brown now looked sable, with copper and bronze highlights that twinkled warmly even in the cold illumination of the room's overhead light. When she reached up to touch it, disbelievingly, she noticed how slender and long her fingers looked.

How could I not have noticed this, her mind screamed. *How could no one else have for that matter? What the hell happened to me that I look like this beautiful stranger?*

Without even knowing what she meant to do, she went in search of the phone and when she found it her fingers immediately dialed the number for the club. Madame Delilah would be there to answer the phone, if no one else was; it was how she'd first made contact with Fetish. What she would say to the Madame, Aerin didn't know, but knew whatever she said, she had to convince the woman to let her speak with Violanti.

But there was no answer tonight. The Madame, it seemed, was out.

She slammed the phone down with a curse.

The doorbell rang. Aerin schooled her features, tried to calm her anger and her confusion, and went to greet her friend. The smile she offered was tight, but Heather didn't seem to notice.

"You won't believe what I did this afternoon," Heather bounded in, breathless.

"What?" Aerin tried to relax, but even the giddy excitement exuding from Heather couldn't set her at ease.

"I turned in my two-week notice. I'm going to be a writer!" Heather promptly threw herself into Aerin's arms and burst into joyous tears.

Aerin hugged her back, softening a little despite her clamoring emotions. "That's wonderful news."

Heather sniffed loudly, grinning through her tears. "Dan sends hugs. He's still kind of surprised that I didn't know he wanted me to write full-time, that it took your suggestion to make me realize it. He's already helping me set up an office, with a new computer and everything. Oh, I'm so happy," she sobbed.

Despite her inner turmoil, Aerin chuckled at the spectacle of this overjoyed woman, who sobbed so messily a spectator might believe she'd just come from a funeral. Aerin offered her a box of tissues and laughed again when Heather loudly blew her nose.

"I'm a goober, I know it. I just can't believe all this is happening, finally happening. Whether I get published or not doesn't matter right now, only that I have the chance to pursue it full-time without having to worry about rent or debts or whatever."

"I'm happy for you," Aerin murmured. And it was true. But there was a selfish part of her that didn't want to see her friend leave, that would miss their shared lunch breaks that had become so dear to her in so short a time. Marriage would likely steal Heather away from her, she'd hardly ever see her after it, and Aerin knew it. But that selfish part of her was easily ignored, and she really *was* happy for her friend.

"Just let me go wash my face and we can go," Heather, who had already familiarized herself with Aerin's small home, hurried to the bathroom even as she spoke the words.

"Heather?" she called out in what she hoped was a nonchalant tone, wondering if it would fool her friend.

"Yeah?" The sound of running water muffled Heather's voice.

"Did you notice my new haircut?" Of course she hadn't had her hair cut, but Aerin wanted to know just how observant her friend was, how drastic her new appearance was to someone close to her.

"Did you get it cut? I'm sorry, I hadn't noticed," she came back into the living room, face rosy and happy. "Your hair grows so fast I guess you have to get it cut pretty often."

So she had noticed something different, at least. She'd noticed that Aerin's hair grew quickly...but what she didn't know was that Aerin's hair had never grown quickly. It had only started that this past month. "Well I didn't really get it cut, I had it styled I guess you could say."

"It looks good. But then it always does. You have great hair, so soft and shiny. It doesn't look any different today though, you must not have had it changed much."

"Yes," she murmured, not really paying attention to what her friend was saying now. She was too busy worrying. *What the hell is happening to me?*

"You seem a little preoccupied tonight."

"Just thinking."

"About what?" Heather pushed, curious as a cat.

"About how much weight I've lost," she said, wondering how far she could go towards mentioning all that was really bothering her without ruining Heather's euphoric mood.

"You mean you haven't checked lately? Your diet's working so well, I'd think you'd be jumping on those scales at least a few times a day. I know I would be. God, if I could shed the pounds as quick as you I'd live on nothing but cream puffs and bon-bons."

"I'm sure I'll gain it all back and be a blubbering whale again in a few short weeks." But did she really believe that? She didn't know what to believe anymore.

Heather snorted. "Don't think that way and don't say that. You were never a blubbering whale. But you have slimmed down a bit and it looks good on you, it really does. You look happier lately. Healthier. So what kind of diet are you on? I admit, I haven't paid much attention to what you've been eating, I've been too self-absorbed with the wedding and quitting my job and all that stuff. Sorry."

"No. Don't be sorry. And I'm not really on any specific kind of diet." Just the kind that made her forget things like the face of her first and only lover, even as she obsessed over him day and night. The kind that made her drop nearly fifty pounds in a month, and one that couldn't be at all good for her heart for both of those reasons. But she felt fine, in fact she felt better than she'd felt in, well, *ever*. "I'm just losing the last of my baby fat," she laughed. She hadn't had any 'baby' fat to lose in over fifteen years.

They turned to leave together, when Heather spotted the painting on the couch. It was so big, Aerin was surprised she'd missed it until now, but then she had been preoccupied.

"Wow, hubba-hubba. This is gorgeous." Heather gasped. "Oh my god, that's you! Who painted this, you naughty girl?"

"The man in the picture." Aerin felt no small amount of pride when she said that. Violanti was as lovely in the painting as he was in real life *and he was her lover*. Wouldn't Heather be shocked? Hell, she was still shocked over the knowledge herself, and she'd been stiff in the saddle for nearly a week as proof of her time spent in his bed.

Heather turned with a puzzled frown. "What man?"

Aerin chuckled over what she assumed was her friend's disbelief. "That man," she reached out and nearly touched the exotic planes of Violanti's bronze face.

Heather's frown deepened. "What are you talking about? This is a picture of you isn't it?"

"Yeah. And the guy who painted it is the guy who's lounging on that bed behind me. His name is —"

"There's no man there, Aerin."

"What? What are you talking about, of course there's a man there," Aerin insisted, incredulous. She put her hand on the painting, tracing the lines of his body, partially hidden in the shadows thrown by her body as they lay there. "He's right here."

"You're teasing me, right?"

"I don't follow you," now it was Aerin's turn to frown.

"I think you need to lie down, Aerin. Something's wrong."

"What are you blind? Can't you see him?"

Tears glinted in Heather's eyes, but they were no longer tears of joy. "There's nobody there, Aerin," she whispered, lips trembling.

"But how can you say that? He's right here," her voice rose shrilly, defensively, as she gesticulated in agitation towards the canvas where Violanti's gaze seemed to burn with a dangerous warning.

Heather backed up, clearly worried and not a little bit frightened. "The only person in that picture is you, hon. Just you. No one else. There's no man painted in it at all."

Chapter Thirteen

Aerin banged fiercely on the door of the club once again, knowing it was no use, that no one would come to answer it.

"God damn it!" she shouted to the empty cobblestone drive that led to the firmly locked oak door. Shielding her eyes against the glare of the late morning sun, she glanced up the towering expanse of stone as if expecting to see someone looking down at her from one of the balconies. If she'd been expecting such a thing, she was sorely disappointed. The mansion seemed deserted.

Well, she hadn't taken the day off from work for nothing, and she certainly wasn't leaving this place before she had some answers to some very important questions.

Like why she was suddenly looking like every young man's wet dream come to life. Or why her memory was full of holes that had everything to do with this strange place. Or why her painting—the lovely painting her gorgeous lover had painted for her—had a ghost in it that no one could see but her.

And she really, really wanted to know why she'd opened her newspaper this morning—as she did on any other normal morning—only to find herself staring at a picture of a man who she'd recently seen in the sitting room of Fetish.

A man who was now mysteriously dead.

The man was one Joseph Tayler. He was the same dark-haired, blue-eyed stranger she'd locked eyes with on her second visit to the club. Poor Mr. Tayler was thought to have been murdered, though there was no real theory yet on just *how* he had been killed. There were no wounds, no bruises, nothing like that to show a violent end. But there had been no blood in his body, absolutely none, and that was strange enough to warrant speculation, none of it pretty.

Tayler's body had been dumped on the doorsteps of his estranged brother's house Sunday morning, but there were no suspects and no leads on how he'd gotten there. Joseph Tayler's death had been too small a story in such a big city to warrant more than a two paragraph article in the local news section of the Thursday morning edition.

But Aerin had noticed it. And Aerin had immediately called in to work, taking the rest of the week off, using two of her many left-over vacation days for 'personal' reasons. She'd needed answers and she'd been bound and determined to get them.

She hadn't reckoned on the place being deserted. On it being as silent as a mausoleum in an ancient graveyard. A foreboding chill shivered up her back, like the caress of a skeleton's finger.

"Fuck the melodrama, just find a way inside stupid," she growled aloud to herself.

The sound of her voice nearly startled her, but it was the impetus she needed to step away from the door and walk the length of the building. It truly was as large as a castle, and she had to wonder just how many rooms the place had. Looking now at the side of the building, which stretched on and on, she knew she'd only seen a small handful of them.

Knocking on the nearest window she called out. "Hello? Is anybody in there?" She pressed her face up to the glass, thankful that the sheer curtains would be easy to see through and beyond into the interior.

"*Shit.*" Choking on a gasp, she stumbled back, tripping and landing on her butt with bruising force.

Unable to believe what she'd just seen, knowing her eyes must be playing horrible tricks on her, she hurriedly regained her feet and looked into the window once again. "Ohmigod, ohmigod, ohmigod."

A crude brick wall completely covered the other side of the window, blocking her view into the house. It had been erected just before the window, close enough to seal off any incoming sunlight, but still far enough away from it that it wasn't easily visible without pressing one's face up against the glass.

But why would anyone brick it up—effectively damaging the overall value of the property—when heavy curtains would have sufficed to dim the harshest rays of the sun?

Perhaps because any sunlight, no matter how dim, was unacceptable to the inhabitants.

The flash of a memory, of Violanti's crimson eyes glowing down at her as he rocked his hips into her body with gentle violence, wrung a cry of panic from her lips. *Get out of here, Aerin, get out of here now!*

But she couldn't. Not without looking in one, two, three more windows. All of them were the same, bricked up solidly against the sun. Breathing in harsh gasps and shaking like a leaf in a storm, she turned in fright and ran back around to the front of the mansion.

There was an iron gate barring the entrance to the courtyard of the club, which doubled as the parking lot, but Aerin had not let it deter her when she entered and she didn't let it deter her now. She slipped through the bars — they were just wide enough to let her newly slender body through, but barely — and sprinted to her car, fumbling with her keys in her haste to flee the premises.

As she drove away she grew calm, her tremors of fear and panic subsiding until she began to wonder just what had spooked her so thoroughly. So she'd seen bricked up windows, big deal, it was a big house and probably drafty with all those windows. Who had designed the windows for that building anyway? It obviously didn't need them if the inhabitants blocked them up like that.

What the fuck is wrong with me? Those windows were bricked up for one reason, and one reason only, to keep out all traces of sunlight! And I know why. Of course I do — after being with Violanti and his glowing chameleon eyes. After reading about Mr. Tayler's blood-drained corpse. Because the people that work and live there are vampires — probably every one of them!

Terror struck her anew and she nearly swerved off the road. Could Violanti be a vampire? More memories assailed her, brought to the surface by her very fear of the possibility, memories of Violanti's mouth at her throat, of the piercing pain and the flowing warmth that followed. Had he drunk her blood? Was it possible? She moaned pitifully.

And almost immediately, as her speeding car put more distance between her and the grounds of Fetish, she calmed down again.

But this time, even as the strange and eerie calm settled over her, her mind could not let go of the image of Violanti's mouth at her throat. Or of the motions his mouth had made as he'd swallowed *something*. And swallowed. And swallowed.

* * * * *

The phone rang, startling Aerin out of her daze. How long had she been sitting there, in the darkness of her living room? She didn't know. Nor did she know how she'd actually made it home after her mad dash from Fetish and all the terrifying questions the morning's journey had raised in her heart and mind. She could remember nothing really, after that morning, so she had probably been sitting here all day, lost in a mindless haze of stillness.

The phone rang again.

Aerin reached over and lifted the receiver, bringing it to her ear with a zombie-like slowness that she couldn't shake.

"Aerin?"

Her heart dropped down into the depths of her icy cold stomach. She swallowed. Hard. "Violanti?"

"I know you were here today."

She swallowed hard around a knot of fear in her throat.

"What happened? Are you hurt?"

"No." Her voice sounded dead, even to her own ears. Even though she knew it would alarm him further, make him wonder, she couldn't prevent it. It didn't matter anyway, from his words it was obvious he already knew she'd been out to the club that day.

"I'm coming over."

"No!"

"I need to explain some things to you. Hiding from me won't help you."

"I'll call the cops, so help me I will. You stay away from me," she shouted into the phone. She'd never spoken to anyone like this in her whole life, and she didn't recognize this violence, this mixture of anger and fear, that swarmed inside her.

"Why would you do that, Aerin? What have I done to frighten you, can you tell me that?"

"You're not...you're not..." her voice shrank to a whisper, "you're not human."

His voice, like velvet, reached out and seemed to stroke over her from head to toe. "Baby, if you told something like that to the police, do you think they'd believe you?"

She gritted her teeth and clenched the phone until she feared it might break in her hands. "What have you done to me?"

"What do you mean? I've done nothing. I wouldn't hurt you, Aerin, you know that. You've been in my arms, in my bed. No matter what you think of me, remember — "

"Shut up," she screamed shrilly. "Don't tell me that, don't say it. I don't want to talk to you. I never want to see you again. *Stay away from me.*"

"You know that's not going to happen." The velvet had turned to steel. "Not now, not ever. You'll have to get used to some things from here on out. I don't know how you found out so much without my telling you, but it's obvious you don't know enough or you wouldn't dare push me like this."

"Are you threatening me?" Her throat was dry as sand.

Velvet crept into his voice again, but the steel was also there, covered by the softness. "Sugar girl, I don't make threats—"

"Then leave me alone," she moaned brokenly.

"—I make promises," he finished. "And I promise you, if you'll just calm down and listen, you'll understand that nothing has changed."

"Everything has changed, you goddamn liar. You've changed me. Everything about me."

"You changed yourself Aerin. I only gave you the power to do it." How still and calm he sounded, how hard and unyielding.

"That accident the other night, the one you left to take care of. That was no accident at all, was it? It was a murder," her voice rose and cracked. "A man died at Fetish Saturday didn't he? And you had something to do with it—"

"I'm coming over."

"No! I'll—I'll kill you if you do, I swear to Christ I will," the sobbing, panicked words tripped over themselves in her haste to say them.

"How?" He sounded unfazed by her threat, merely curious.

"Fuck you, Violanti! Fuck you, don't you come over here."

The phone clicked in her ear. Deafening silence came through the line.

With a wild cry, she raced through the house, locking her doors and windows, even as she was blinded by angry, terrified tears.

She had no gun, no weapon, save a butcher knife which she grabbed from a drawer in her kitchen. Turning on every light in every room she tried to think of some plan to keep Violanti away. She knew she couldn't call the cops and tell them her wild tale of vampires and murder and sex. No one would believe her, and if she was lucky they would simply ignore her and not lock her away in some lunatic asylum. She was on her own.

Left to face the devil or vampire or whatever he was.

"Wait a minute. If he's a vampire, he can't come in here unless I invite him, right?" She thought back over the years, trying to remember every vampire movie she'd ever forced herself to sit through, every horror story she'd ever dared to pick up and read on the subject. She was certain that the one cardinal rule in just about all those tales of the macabre was that vampires could not enter a home without the owner's permission.

Hysterical, triumphant laughter exploded from her lips. She'd just sit here and wait him out. He'd never get an invitation from her, no matter how long he knocked on her door. For all she cared he could rot out there on her doorstep. She wasn't letting anyone in her house tonight.

Chapter Fourteen

Sometime during her long midnight vigil she must have fallen asleep. And she was having such a delicious dream she didn't want to think about waking up from it.

Cool silken lips danced over the thin cotton of her tank top. The tip of a wicked tongue wet the hard stab of her nipple before the mouth drew it in, sucking it gently.

Fingers cupped and squeezed the mound of her sex through her boxer shorts, a flimsy barrier against such sensual determination. Aerin moaned and let the dream take her deeper…

Violanti smiled against her nipple, knowing she slept too deeply to awaken. He wouldn't let her awaken. He liked her just as she was here, dreaming in his arms, no longer scared or frightened, but open fully to his touch like a blooming flower in the heat of a dewy summer morning.

Her mouth parted on another moan, drawing his eyes. Oh the things he wanted to do to her mouth—and would do before the night was through. So she knew his secrets now—some of them anyway—he didn't care. For the first time in five centuries a human knew who and what he was and he cared nothing but that she did not turn away from him. That she did not flee.

All it would take was a little convincing, he was sure, to keep her from bolting. She was in thrall to his sensuality, to his charm, and he would use that against her like a weapon until he got what he wanted.

But what did he want from her? Ultimately, he did not know. It bemused and perhaps alarmed him a little, this strange uncertainty in him, but that didn't matter. He'd been playing with fire from the first moment he'd locked gazes with this woman. He'd upped the ante by giving her his painting, knowing it would release her from the spell of forgetfulness he'd laid over Fetish whenever she caught sight of it. He'd known she would suspect something sooner or later after receiving that gift, after accepting it into her home.

And as she'd accepted that gift, so too had she unwittingly invited him into her home, something he knew she'd been smart enough to determine not to do tonight, for not all Hollywood fictions were far from the mark. It was why she'd waited up for him instead of fleeing. Waiting with that paltry and insufficient weapon clenched tightly in her hands, until he'd sent her into a deep sleep and carried her easily to bed. Tonight, he vowed, he would show her how useless all her defenses were against him, and in doing so he would also put an end to her unfounded fear of him.

And she would love every hot and sticky minute of it.

His sugar girl was no dim-witted human, even if she was a little naïve. Her discovery of his nature—or at least the gist of it—had proven that much. And after their conversation on the phone—if that farce of an argument could indeed be called one—it was abundantly clear that she was no longer timid or shy. She'd actually had the courage to tell him to shut up. Hell, she'd screamed it at him. No one had ever commanded him to do anything, let alone to shut up. She had changed in so many ways from the frightened innocent he'd first met.

It was so endearingly irritating. Everything about her was, and it made him hard as a rock knowing he'd helped her spread her wings as well as her legs.

Moving up he kissed her on the mouth, hard. Gods but she had the most fuckable mouth he'd ever seen.

She was a menace.

He'd be wise to get up, wipe her memory clean, take his painting, and leave. But he knew he couldn't. No more than he could kill her without killing himself. He loved her too damn much.

And when had he come to love her?

From the first night, when she'd eaten him with her innocent eyes as he'd shot his load all over his stomach? She'd been breathless, trembling. And so wetly aroused he'd actually smelled the faint traces of blood from her most recent menses there in the heat between her legs. Oh yes, he'd loved her even then, and had known full well he was doomed to tell her everything sooner or later, whether she wanted to listen or not.

He knew he would have to let her awaken. Knew, too, that he'd have to overcome her anger and her fear before he could accomplish anything further in their relationship. But first…her mouth drew his eyes and he licked his lips like the dangerous predator he was.

The long fingers of his hand went to the fastening of his pants and Aerin sighed deeply in her sleep.

* * * * *

"Wake up Aerin. It's time to talk."

Cold water couldn't have made her gasp awake faster than those smiling words from Violanti's mouth. With a shriek she backed up on the bed. Her mouth was full of an odd lingering sweetness, her head was dizzy, and she wondered how in the hell she'd ended up in the bed with him when only minutes ago—

"You made me sleep."

Those sinful lips of his stretched in a wide, wicked grin. "I did."

"You broke into my house."

"Yes." The grin broadened, blazing with teeth that glinted in the moonlight. He'd turned the light off in her room, she realized, thought it didn't seem important in that moment. He'd probably done it to put her off balance.

When her eyes fully focused in the dark—where were her contacts?—she realized that he was deliciously rumpled as he lounged there next to her. His pants were open, his cock—shiny and wet and hard—jutted up towards his navel, and his shirt was pulled high on his stomach.

"What did you do?" Her mouth tingled.

"What do you mean?"

His wide-eyed innocence didn't fool her for a second. The sweet flavor that lingered on her tongue seemed suddenly significant. "Why do you look like that?" she motioned towards his dishevelment.

"Why do you think?" Such a wickedly sinuous voice, it made her crazy with lust, even though she fought like hell against it.

Her mouth felt swollen, sexy, bruised. That, combined with the lingering flavor in her mouth…and she knew exactly what he'd been up to.

"You pig! I was *asleep*," she screeched with indignation even as she savored the wild taste of him, and savor it she did, despite the circumstances and despite herself.

He laughed. "So? I wasn't. And you liked it," he leaned conspiratorially closer, eyes glowing in the moonlight that shone through the window of her bedroom, "you moaned around me."

"In disgust!"

"Liar. You gulped me down like a woman dying of thirst. You licked me with that long tongue of yours, purring like a kitten with each spurt."

"Why you *jerk*—" She launched herself at him, beyond fear, pissed as hell over his sheer, unrepentant gall.

He let her hit him, laughing like a loon in a carefree way she'd never heard from him before. Not even trying to dodge her blows, as if her slapping and punching him didn't hurt at all.

And then she realized it probably didn't. Not if he was a vampire. He was too strong for that.

She stilled, her veins chilling to ice. "Did you come here to kill me?"

He sobered instantly. "Don't be stupid. I could have killed you a thousand times by now and you know it."

"So why didn't you?" She sank back, eyeing him warily.

His impatient glare was so filled with exasperation she wanted to punch him again, and would have, if she'd thought it would faze him any. "You know why, you just don't want to accept it. I'm no killer, Aerin."

"But you are a vampire. Aren't you?" Never in a million years would she have imagined she'd be having a conversation like this, across from a man who was naked and sensuously replete from his moonlight molestations. It was all too absurd. She almost laughed, but didn't, because she knew it would sound hysterical.

His eyes shimmered in the dim light, from silver to blue to green to bright and burning crimson and she knew he did it on purpose. To drive the point home, as it were. "I am. But not like your normal, Hollywood vampire." His hand moved down over his cock, toying with the silver bar that pierced his still-hardened flesh.

She tried to look away—knew it was a hopeless endeavor—so instead watched his every move with growing excitement despite her fear.

"Isn't silver bad for vampires or something?" she asked, her mouth dry and her voice raspy.

His eyes were devilish and knowing. "I guess you could say I'm allergic to silver. It burns," his fingers tugged gently on the silver bar and his breath hissed between his teeth, "quite a lot." The head of his cock wept a lone tear of arousal. "I love the small pain; it heightens my pleasure."

Aerin took a deep, unsteady breath. She tried to remember why they were here, why they were having this conversation. Tried with all her might to ignore her own needs, her own arousal. "If you're not like a Hollywood vampire then what are you like?" She had to know.

His fingers stilled on himself and he straightened his clothes decisively. Aerin could have wept when he refastened his trousers. "Will you listen? Truly listen to what I have to say?" he asked.

"Yes. Just tell me."

"Very well then, Aerin my love. I'll tell you what I have never told another human being for over five hundred years…"

Chapter Fifteen
Florence, Italy
1497

"Violanti, stupid boy, bring me the egg yolks — and hurry."

Violanti's mouth twisted in a fury. He was no longer a boy — not at twenty three — but his master insisted on calling him that and would until he either died or Violanti killed him. And Violanti D'Arco knew he just might do it, he was that fed up with the old man's incessant demands.

After all, his name meant, loosely, violent darkness. It was his nature, after all, to eventually wreak havoc in some fashion. Hadn't his drunken louse of a father told him so time after time, more often with his booted foot than not? If anyone would know of that violence in his heart it would have been his father, who'd had the same dark blood.

The D'Arco family was descended from sorcerers, practitioners of the black arts that dated back to Merlin himself. Or so the stories went.

It should be little surprise to anyone that he harbored such dangerous thoughts as beating his master to death. But he wouldn't do it. He knew he wouldn't. He'd grit his teeth, bury his anger, and see to the old man's demands.

Violanti did want to become his own master, after all, and the only way to do that was to stay with this master and learn the last lessons that would perfect his art. He'd been learning his whole life, studying and producing, but his present master—a student of Lorenzo the Great—would teach him things no school, text, or teacher could have taught him before now. It was why he'd come here three years ago at the advanced age of twenty, to this city so far from his rural ancestral home, to learn from one of the greatest painters in Florence.

Painting was the only thing that mattered to Violanti. Painting and women. And he was a gifted artist with both mediums. He'd been painting all his life, had been bedding women since his thirteenth birthday, and here, at last, was his chance to perfect both skills. Here, in the epicenter of renaissance learning that was Florence.

"Hurry up boy," the old man growled again, impatient and scowling.

Violanti gritted his teeth and did as his master bid him, opening his mind to receive the lesson he would learn as the old man set brush to canvas in the sultry summer air of the *palazzo*.

Hours later, as the sun sank down over, Violanti looked at the fruits of his labor. A vibrant painting, a scene of plump female statues rendered in marble among an overgrowth of twisting vines and broken pottery. The piece would please his patroness, and Violanti would earn many *florins* for the effort. He was pleased. It was not yet perfection, not yet good enough to appease his demanding thirst for excellence, but it was close enough for now.

"You will take it to the *Signora* tonight."

Violanti frowned. "It is not yet dry. It will take many days for the pigments to set—"

"I know this boy, but she has commanded that it be delivered the very night it is finished and no later."

Well the rich and pompous noblewoman who had commissioned the piece could have it whenever she wanted, so long as she paid Violanti the coins she had promised. He grunted his assent to the old man, who scowled at what he no doubt found intolerable insolence in an apprentice. "I will take it to her," Violanti murmured.

"After the sun has set and no sooner."

Of course, he remembered the Signora's eccentric request that their business be done in only the moonlit hours of the night. How could he dare forget with such a ripe purse involved? As the sun set over the horizon he gathered his precious cargo and made for the *Signora's* home.

Walking the streets of Florence in the hours of the night was an experience Violanti greatly enjoyed. So many different walks of life mingled here, in search of knowledge, in search of art. Politics were discussed openly and heatedly, the lifeblood of the city. Poetry and song filled the air. Food and wine flowed; pretty women spread their legs eagerly for any man with traces of paint under his nails. It was a lovely, magical place, Florence.

"Hello, beautiful one," a sultry voice called to him from a doorway.

"Maria, my flower."

The woman laughed, sashaying over to him with a promising smile on her lips. "Did you think to slink past me without my notice? You devil. I am not so easily tricked." Maria sighed and licked her lips like the wanton she was. "I am hot for you tonight, my stallion. Will you not join me for an hour?"

Violanti, careful of the painting, kissed her hard on the lips with gallant flair. "Not now my flower. I have a painting to deliver to its new owner, and it cannot wait."

Her hooded gaze lit up with a sudden fire, glancing towards the canvas he held so protectively. "Can I see—?"

He stepped back. "No. It is still wet. I hold it over my head, see," his hands tightened, "so that the paint does not smudge or run."

She pouted, and Violanti had to admit that it was a luscious pout indeed. "You are cruel, Violanti. I love your paintings, but you do not share this one with me. You owe me greatly for that," she teased. "You'll come back tonight?"

"I'll come back," he promised, not knowing then that he would never see the lovely Maria again.

"Kiss me again so I will believe you."

He did, opening his mouth for her tongue, feeling his cock grow hard with the promise in that kiss. Breaking away wasn't too difficult, but it wasn't entirely easy either.

With a jaunty swing in his step he made his way at last to the *Signora's* house. It was dark inside, unlike the thousands of other homes that lit up the night with their numerous emblazoned candles. He wondered idly if she was home, he did not want to have to carry the painting back to the *palazzo*. He wanted to stop and spend an hour—or three—in the arms of the luscious Maria.

"*Buon giorno, Signora* Laggia. *Buon giorno, palazzo* Laggia. Is anyone home?"

There was no answer. But a warm and languid feeling was seeping over his body, not unlike the sweet heat of desire. "Hello," he called again, surprised that his voice could sound so faint. So far away.

A light glinted suddenly in the window, beckoning him forward.

It was dark inside the house. Violanti carefully placed the painting of Greco styled sculptures before the hearth. A noise behind him made him start and whip around.

"You startled me, *Signora*."

"Did I, *Signore* D'Arco?" Her voice was just as husky, just as magical and arousing as he'd remembered.

"*Si*. You did."

"Then I apologize." The flickering light of the candelabra she held cast eerie but beautiful shadows across her face.

For some reason he couldn't explain, he felt cornered, trapped by her glittering gaze. And it was in no way unpleasant. He was hard as marble because of it. "I have brought your painting."

"And you will no doubt be wanting your fee, will you not my beautiful *artista*?"

He was drowning in her eyes. Her hand, so cool and so soft, floated up to caress his whisker-roughened face.

"So much talent in one so very, very young. Do you like this life, Violanti? Do you like being the servant to a senile old man who has not half the talent that lies dormant and sleeping inside of you?"

Startled, uneasy, he swallowed as her mouth moved close to him. He almost lost control, almost spilled his seed then and there.

"You have so much potential. If only you knew. If only you had the time to find it within yourself..."

"W-what are you doing *Signora*?"

"I am lonely and weary and spent. But you are full of fire and passion. I would borrow these things from you. Do you want me Violanti D'Arco, son of sorcerers, child of man, master of painters?" Her gaze burned.

His ego swelled along with his cock, even as his mouth filled with the metallic taste of fear. He could not lie to her, could not find the will to try. "Yes."

"Will you share your sex with me?"

Her hand cupped him tenderly and he fell to his knees with a moan. She followed him down with an enigmatic smile. "Y-yes."

"Will you share blood with me?"

In that moment she could have asked him anything and he would have answered yes. "Yes."

"Will you share long years with me? Learn from me until you are strong enough to go out and taste the world on your own? A master of your own fate."

What was she asking him? She had somehow removed all their clothing without his notice, without his help, and was moving to straddle his pulsing, aching cock. "Yes. Yes to everything. Yes a thousand times," he babbled as she sank down over him like a wet and burning glove.

Signora Laggia smiled, revealing a set of wicked, sharp incisors. And then she struck.

And Violanti's fate was sealed. He was a living man no more, in thrall to the woman that took him and made of him an incubus. A being of blood and passion, immortal and beautiful forever. He loved every second of his death, screaming his ecstasy to the heavens, and was reborn into the long years of forever.

Chapter Sixteen

"So you feed on sex and on blood."

"Yes. And those things must be given freely or it has no lasting value."

"Like fast food compared to a gourmet feast, huh?"

He smiled, leaning back against the wall as if tired after telling her his story. "Something like that."

"What happened to the woman who made you, *Signora* Laggia?"

"She tired of me quickly, and I of her. We were both too independent to stay long with each other, too stubborn, too intent on our own pleasures."

"Did you love her?"

"She was my mother. My lover. She is still my friend, though I have not heard or spoken to her in almost a century."

"You didn't answer me."

"You sound jealous," he teased. "Are you?"

"Just answer the damn question."

"No one who could hear you now would believe that but a month ago you were timid as a mouse."

"Arrrrgh!" she exclaimed in exasperation.

Violanti laughed. "Calm yourself. No. I did not love her. I do not love her. Our tie to one another is not so strong or complicated as that."

They fell silent for a long, long while.

"What happened to Joseph Tayler?" She had to know, had to hear it from his own lips. She would believe him, no matter what he said.

There was no pretense between them now. He didn't even bother to pretend he didn't know who she was talking about. "Mr. Tayler was bled dry by his lover, a fledgling at the club who knew no better and had no self-control. He died as well — trapped in death with his human lover."

"You had nothing to do with it?"

"I gave the order to dispose of their bodies. And instructions that Mr. Tayler was to be left with a bag of nearly half a million dollars to be shared among any surviving family or friends he might have. But I did not kill either of them."

A half a million dollars! She hadn't read about that in the paper. No doubt the brother had conveniently forgotten to mention its existence to the authorities. "Wait a minute. *You* gave the order?"

"Yes."

"And Madame Delilah, did she know about this?"

"You are full of foolish questions tonight, my love. Yes Delilah knew about it. Yes she helped to carry out my orders."

"But why would she do that?"

Violanti shot her a puzzled stare, then laughed, obviously realizing what was causing her such confusion. "Because I am the master of Fetish. Everyone who lives within the club owes their livelihoods, indeed their very lives, to me. They all do as I say, without question."

"You own the club?" She felt like a parrot.

"Yes."

"That's why Delilah didn't charge me for my visits, not even that first time."

"You checked, did you?" His eyes twinkled. "Yes that is why. Though we do not, as a rule, charge our clients after the first visit anyway. Not in dollars. We charge the price of passion and blood. It is worth far more than money to us anyway. For you, I waived the monetary fee entirely. What I took from you was far too precious to put a price on."

Aerin ignored that. "What about the painting? My best friend thinks my menopausal hormones have made me crazy, because I can see a man in that painting who she insists isn't there. Why can't anyone see you in it but me?"

"Because I willed it so. I mixed my blood into the pigments of the paint and in doing so placed a spell over it. That painting enabled you to remember things about me and about Fetish, but it also prevented others from seeing too clearly the secrets that must be kept from strangers. My very existence is secret; no human outside the club must recognize me or any other members of my coven. It is a necessary precaution. We are not human. If our existence were discovered, it would bring total chaos."

Her breathing quickened, coming in short, panicked, jerky breaths. "I can't believe this is happening."

Violanti reached out to her, putting his hands gently on her shoulders. "Breathe slowly. You're hyperventilating."

"I know that, you butthead!" The anger helped to calm her panic somewhat, but her lungs still shuddered with every breath she took.

The shock in his eyes might have, under different circumstances, made her laugh.

"No one has ever called me a butthead before," he said the word with a hint of a sneer, as if the very feel of that word on his lips was abhorrent.

"Well you are one. A big fat, hairy, smelly, butthead."

The long dark veil of his lashes twitched with his shock. He blinked several times before speaking again. "Are you feeling better yet?"

"Yes."

"I love you, you know," he said bluntly.

Aerin mewled, panic swamping her again. "No you don't."

He merely looked at her.

"You're a vampire!"

"An incubus. Wait, no, that's not entirely accurate either. Technically I'm neither vampire nor incubus, those are merely terms thought up by humans to classify something that is beyond mere mortal comprehension. I simply am what I am."

"Let's not quibble over semantics. You've bitten me. Drunk my blood. I know you have. That makes you a vampire, your drinking my blood."

His gaze burned hot and bright, crimson pinpoints in the darkness. "And it was sweeter than any I have ever tasted."

"I don't love you," she blurted out.

"You're a terrible liar," he said with a wry twist of his lips.

"I do *not* love you!" She punched him in the arm without even knowing she'd meant to make the move.

He sighed. "Whether you admit to loving me or not, you now have a choice to make, sugar girl."

A zing of fear stung her into immobility. "Oh yeah? W-what is that?"

"Whether you will accept me. Accept what I am. And all that it means. Or whether I wipe your memory clean of me, of Fetish and all who dwell within it, and let you die a natural death, unaware of these events."

"I don't understand. Why can't I just promise not to tell anyone? And what do you mean by a natural death, will you kill me otherwise?"

"If you choose to turn away from me I will take the memory of me and mine from you, I will not jeopardize my coven out of love, not even for you. But if you should take me, accepting all of me, then I shall take your mortal death from you and make you my wife. Something I have never attempted with another in all my years, never thought to. You will be the first and only for me. My child of the blood. I will give you everlasting life, and stay by your side forever."

Aerin flew from the bed, but Violanti was too quick for her, moving faster than her sight could follow, grabbing her to him. He brought her back against him, his mouth pressing a fevered kiss to her neck. She moaned, whether in fear or desire she wasn't sure. If she were honest with herself she would have to admit that it was a potent mixture of both. His hand cupped her breast firmly. He let her feel the dangerous scrape of his teeth over her pulse.

"You don't fear me, sugar girl. You fear yourself and what your own passions will make you do," he growled.

"Let go of me."

"Don't fear me. I would never willingly hurt you. You know that. Why continue this fight?"

"Because I'm confused! Because less than a month ago I was a fat, middle-aged virgin who cowered at the very idea of changing any of those things. Now look at me. Just look at me! Look at what you've done to me," she spun in his arms and he let her, railing at him in anger and desperation.

"You are beautiful. As you have always been beautiful. Whatever magic was mine to give, I gave freely to you in our nights spent together, so that you could find in your body the beauty to match that which was already there, but that you never could see. The beauty I have always seen and desired in you."

"I was never beautiful. I am now but this isn't me, this body isn't mine."

"But it is. It is the blooming of your confidence, of your sensuality, your womanly power that you see now in the mirror when you care to look. My magic only gave you the knowledge of those tools needed to bring about such change. My power did not give you the tools themselves. They were always there, inside of you."

"I don't know if I love you or hate you, damn it."

"I will give you until Saturday to think on it, since you don't know your own mind. Be at Fetish Saturday night with your decision." At last a trace of anger stained his tone, but his face remained impassive.

"That's not long enough."

"It will have to be, sugar girl. Like it or not, until Saturday is as long as I can give you. Think about it. You can have an eternity with me, or you can lose about four weeks worth of your memory. It's your choice."

He seemed to vanish before her eyes and it was only the slam of her front door that convinced her he didn't have the power to appear and disappear at whim. He didn't have to. He moved that fast.

"Damn you, you...*vampire*! *Arrrgh.*"

Chapter Seventeen

Saturday came and went, and Aerin let it go with hardly a qualm. She didn't go to Fetish. She didn't leave her house. She wanted to see just what Violanti would do if she failed to show up at the club as he'd so arrogantly commanded her to do.

She was surprised when he didn't do anything.

There were no phone calls, no visits, nothing. Just an endless, foreboding silence. It made her uneasy. But it also relieved her a little. She'd needed more time to think things through.

Taking the week off of work was easy. Even Heather had encouraged the decision, still believing her friend to be overworked and overstressed after the debacle of the painting. Aerin wondered if things would ever be the same between them. She wondered if it even mattered. If Violanti had his way she'd either be with him forever or lose a chunk of her memory, and either scenario didn't allow much room for Heather's friendship in her life, no matter how much she might have wanted it otherwise.

Things were rapidly spiraling out of control and there was nothing Aerin could do to prevent that.

Her emotions were so convoluted and confused, she didn't know up from down. For days she paced the rooms of her house, thinking about everything and nothing, wondering when, and if, Violanti would come. She wondered if she wanted him to come. With something like horror, she realized that she did, more than anything. That realization scared the living daylights out of her.

She was in love with the vampire.

But was she ready to give up her life for him? To spend forever with him? He'd promised her forever. She believed he'd keep that promise. And while an eternity spent in the arms of her true love might seem magical and right on the surface, she feared the current that flowed underneath it all.

If she chose to stay with him, she would become like him. She would have to drink blood. She would have to feed on pleasure—what had Violanti called it, that golden energy that spilled out from humans when they shared sex? Life force. She would have to take the life force from humans in order to live. But could she actually, in good conscience, do something like that?

Round and round her thoughts raced. She couldn't eat, could hardly sleep—too many dreams—all she could do was think.

And stare at Violanti's painting.

For hours on end she would sit in her living room, staring at that canvas with a dreamy smile on her face. Sometimes she could swear that Violanti's eyes were really looking out at her from it, that he could see her sitting there from wherever he may be. Aerin supposed it wasn't impossible. She'd seen and learned so many amazing things ever since meeting Violanti, she wouldn't have put this bit of magic past him even for a second.

All this thinking and wondering was doing her no good, though she'd hoped for the time in which to indulge her convoluted thoughts. She kept coming back to the realization that perhaps there really wasn't a choice for her at all, perhaps there never had been, not from the first moment she'd locked gazes with the master of Fetish.

It was Thursday night before she heard anything. And it wasn't Violanti who sought her out. It was Madame Delilah.

Aerin was shocked to see the woman waiting patiently for her to open the door and admit her inside. She would have expected anyone but her.

"May I come in?"

Wordlessly, Aerin nodded.

The Madame chuckled. "It doesn't work that way. You have to say it out loud. Or you have to take something of mine, but I'm afraid I have nothing to give you."

"Come in."

With elegant grace the taller woman stepped across the threshold and moved deeper into Aerin's house, projecting a serene calmness that somehow managed to set Aerin at ease. "You have a lovely home," the Madame said after looking carefully about the room. "I haven't been in the dwelling of a human since the 1940's, when I was a human myself."

Aerin started. "That long?"

Delilah smiled, "Oh yes."

"How," Aerin swallowed, "how did you become...what you are?"

"My lover. He fell in love with me and I with him. We could not bear to be parted. And so he made me what he was, so that I might live with him forever."

"Where is he now?" Surely here would be the answer that would sway her decision one way or another. In so many books the vampire easily tired of his lover, and eternity was a very long time to share with any one person.

"He lives at Fetish, helping me keep the house accounts, as in love with me as I am with him. Our passions and our hearts have never weakened for one another." Delilah laughed. "You look surprised at that. Don't you think we immortals have any staying power in our hearts? Are you worried that Violanti will tire of you, is that it?"

The woman could undoubtedly read minds. "I am," Aerin admitted, sitting down hard on her sofa.

The Madame joined her, graceful in every move she made. "Don't be. Violanti is one of those rare beings among us who can only give his heart once. It's why he's never brought another human into the blood, he can't give immortality without giving himself in the bargain. He's waited a long time for you. Too long," her eyes held censure, no doubt because Aerin was dragging her feet over the whole affair.

"I can't eat people. I just can't."

"You don't eat anything, stupid." The insult sounded so strange and yet so easy on the woman's elegantly painted lips. "Human's are not cattle to us, no matter what popular literature has led you to believe. They are sensual creatures, sacred and sweet. We do feed on them, or rather on their more than ample life force, on their sex, and on their blood. There is nothing shameful or wrong in it. They are willing or we do not bother."

"But they are not aware. It's the same as stealing."

"You know nothing of which you speak. You merely assume. We do not force anyone to come to Fetish. They come of their own free will. And whatever we take from them is returned tenfold. We give sex and we give pleasure, and in cases like yours, when you first came to us, we give hope. You cannot lie to me and say you haven't benefited from knowing us."

"You're right. But that doesn't mean I could live like you do. I couldn't share Violanti with anyone, I couldn't be with anyone but him. I would accept nothing less than monogamy between us, I couldn't."

"Can I taste you," she asked bluntly.

"I am not food," Aerin scooted away from her.

"No you are not. But I will show you that you can feed on humans without 'sharing' yourself or Violanti in the way you assume. Allow me to show you this. Please?"

Without waiting for her assent, Delilah moved closer, putting her arms around her gently. The woman's lips were cool on her cheek, friendly. "I won't hurt you."

"You all keep saying that, but it doesn't make things any easier for me."

Delilah snorted her laughter. "Just one small taste. Violanti would allow me that under the circumstances, I think," she murmured.

Aerin felt dizzy. Suddenly drunk and languid and totally at ease. "What are you doing to me?"

"Tasting you."

"I don't understand."

"You will." The Madame pressed her forehead lightly against Aerin's shoulder.

Warm, languid pleasure seeped into the very marrow of her bones. Delicious and lovely, but in no way was it threatening or overly sexual. It felt wonderful and rejuvenating, a sweet relief to Aerin, who hadn't slept in days and was completely exhausted.

Delilah reached for her hand, raising her wrist to cool, silken lips. A deep, sharp sting signaled her bite and Aerin cried out softly. But she had no strength or will to fight. A tiny sip and it was done. The warm breath of the Madame closed the tiny wounds, healing them, and Aerin came back to herself with a calm she hadn't felt in days.

"That was but a small taste, but after many such sips from different people who are more than willing to share, it is more than enough for us. And it does not compromise our bonds with our mates in any way. You have nothing to fear on that score, you see?"

"This is so strange."

"Life is always strange. For us, as well as humans. Really, we're not too dissimilar from each other in many respects. Some of us are good, some of us are bad; we have our weaknesses and our strengths. We love. Oh, how we of the blood can love. Perhaps more passionately even than humans, who are notorious for the strength of their hearts."

"Where is Violanti? Why hasn't he come?"

The Madame's eyes shadowed. "He is even more stubborn than you are. I thought he would tear the place apart when you failed to come Saturday night. He has confined himself to his rooms and will not speak to us. I think he's waiting for you to make the first move. But I knew you needed a push, whether Violanti approved or not, and so I came."

"I don't know what to do," she pushed up the rims of her glasses nervously — one of her contact lenses had been lost the day of her trip to Fetish and she hadn't bothered ordering a replacement.

"Decide. Choose between an immortal life of love with Violanti and a mortal life of short, lonely years without him. And without the memory of him to comfort you. For though Violanti may not have the heart to follow through with taking your memories from you, I can assure you I have no such qualms."

Aerin shuddered, hearing the cold hard will in Delilah's cultured tones, knowing she would make good on her promise without hesitation. "I need time."

"Time is something you don't have anymore. You've already taken far too much. I will give you until tomorrow night. The doors of Fetish will open to you then, and you can come to Violanti to either start your life together or sever ties completely. It's all up to you, my dear girl. I hope you're brave enough to make that choice. I don't want to have to chase you down."

As a dare, it worked to make Aerin's stubborn streak rear its head defiantly. As a threat it also succeeded, and a chill of fear made her shiver.

"I'll be there tomorrow night."

Delilah smiled. "I knew you would be."

Chapter Eighteen

The door was red. As dark and deep a ruby hue as a pool of shimmering blood. This door led, Delilah assured her, to Violanti's private apartment. His home.

She thought to knock, but decided against it. Let him be surprised, if it were possible, when she simply walked through his door. That is, if it wasn't locked against her.

It wasn't.

The apartment was designed as exquisitely as the rest of the mansion. Red and gold and dark rich woods abounded, among lush fabrics and textures that welcomed and lured and relaxed her. A large living room led to a small kitchen — though what a vampire might need with one, Aerin had no idea — and on into the back of the home was another door, opened to admit her into the expansive bedroom.

"Violanti?" His room was full of shadows. Only candlelight burned here, warm and seductive, and she did not see him at first as he sat in dim flickers of light. Though how she could have missed him on the incredibly large bed, she had no idea. He was lounging there, looking at her with a lazy gaze that burned her from head to toe.

The bed was as large as her entire bedroom, and how Violanti could have found bedding for it was an amazing feat. But then, he was no doubt wealthy enough to afford specially made linens. Or silks, as the case may be, for that was what covered the bed now. Silks and satins and furs in tones of gold, black, and crimson. The same colors of his skin, hair, and eyes.

He was deliciously nude.

"Why have you come," he sounded belligerent. He wasn't going to make this easy for her. "Go away. While I can still let you."

"No."

He rose on the bed, draping his arms on his bent knees with negligent grace.

"Why are you here?" he asked again.

The moment of truth, of courage. And she wondered why the hell she'd been so long in coming here after all.

"Why have you come? I want nothing more to do with you." He ran a hand through his hair, every move as erotic as a kiss.

"You're lying," she said, softly, "you wanted me here, so I came."

"You are late. I told you, if you did not come on Saturday, that I would be forced to wipe away your memory of me. And so I shall," he bit out the last.

"Don't." She hated to hear the iron hard finality in his voice. Hated to think he might be telling the truth, that he wouldn't give her another chance. "Please don't."

He was before her in a flash, she blinked and she missed his move. His fingers bit into her chin as he held her face still for his perusal. "Tell me why I shouldn't."

"I'm here now. I came," she stated.

"No. Tell me why you're here." His face leaned towards hers, but his gaze and his voice never once softened.

"You still love me," she said, though a twinge of doubt darkened her heart.

"I shouldn't," he said, and she nearly shouted with relief. But he dashed that relief almost at once when he added, "And it changes nothing."

"Please," she trembled.

"Please what?" His fingers nearly bruised her.

"I'm sorry."

"So am I. Sorry that you are too afraid to know your own heart, sorry that I cannot let you remember how close you came to true happiness."

"Violanti, don't say that. You love me."

"And you love me," his hand fell to her shoulder and shook her until her teeth rattled, "say that you love me and all *might* be forgiven."

"No," she protested, afraid of this violence in him. She *did* love him, she knew it, but to give him the words and have him still decide to abandon her and take her memory would have killed her on the spot.

"Say it, damn you," his fingers did bruise her now, digging in brutally. His eyes flashed crimson and his mouth was a tight, pale line. "Why are you here? Tell me why you're here."

A traitorous sob escaped her. "Because I love you," she managed to whisper.

Violanti flung away from her, retreating back to the bed. Her heart cracked as he turned his back on her.

"I love you Violanti," she said again, louder this time.

He turned back to look at her coolly. Aerin felt as if her world was ending. Tears filled her eyes. With a painful finality, she knew he would not relent. He would take her memory from her. She had waited too long, gambled too dearly, and now she would lose him forever.

"Please Violanti. Don't be like this," she sobbed, "I'm sorry I didn't come. But I was scared. I didn't know what to do, what to think. Haven't you ever been afraid?"

His lashes widened, his gaze flared bright and hot. "Come here."

Terrified, knowing it was foolish, she moved to do so.

"Wait."

She stopped, tears falling unchecked now, wondering at his command.

"Take off your clothes first."

Her breath shuddered. She did as she was told. His eyes followed her every move, drinking in the hardened stab of her nipples, the slope of her belly, the cleanly shaved mound of her pussy.

Aerin climbed on the bed, crawling towards him.

"Stop weeping and lie back," he commanded coolly.

"I trust you Violanti," she whispered, shaking, lying down on the cool satin sheets. "I love you. I'll always love you, even if you take yourself from my memory. I'll always remember you, deep down. I'll always know that you love me too," she choked, crying openly and without shame, believing that every word she spoke was true. Hoping that he would believe in them too.

There was only a slight hesitation in her now. She trusted him, knew he loved her, knew she loved him in return. No magic could erase that truth.

"Spread your legs."

She did, wide, knowing he watched her.

Long, long moments passed. Aerin's heart raced. Violanti made no move towards her, but she could feel his desire. It enveloped the room, heating it. She knew his eyes were roving over her naked, quivering flesh, knew he was aching to pounce.

"Say it again," he said at last. "Say you love me."

She smiled amidst her tears, hoping for his mercy. "I do love you. Now and forever."

"Forever is what I want from you," he said thickly. His hands reached out and tenderly wiped her tears away. "Have you decided then? Will you be with me or no?"

He wasn't going to take the choice from her, her heart rejoiced in the knowledge. She swallowed a giddy laugh of relief and focused instead on his presence, on his question. There was no turning back from this choice, there never had been. "I will be with you," she promised, and it felt perfect, it felt right.

"Take off your glasses. You won't need them anymore."'

She did, throwing them negligently to the far side of the bed, where they bounced, slid, and fell to the floor with a dull clunk.

"Spread your legs wider."

Shivering, excited now, she obeyed.

He covered her, jarring her with his eagerness to trap her there beneath him. Without even touching her, she was wet and ready, and he slipped fully into her. "Tonight's lesson is lovemaking."

More tears sprang to her eyes, as he slowly, silently loved her. His kisses covered her face, her neck, her breasts. There was no inch of her body that his hands did not touch and caress. Warm liquid pleasure drowned her.

Moaning, reaching, she wrapped her legs around him, meeting his every move with one of her own.

They danced together, joined as one, the loving so sweet and so total that soon Aerin was crying from the beauty of it.

"Shh, sugar girl. Don't cry," he drank her tears, sipping them delicately from the shell of her eyelids, "I'm sorry I scared you. I was angry. You dared to disobey me."

"I'm sorry, too." She clutched him tighter, desperate. "Don't leave me. Don't ever take this from me."

"Never," he swore, thrusting deep.

"I do love you," she had to say it, had to tell him.

"I know."

She bit him for that. His chuckle changed to a groan. He thrust his cock harder into her wet body. Deep. "Do that again."

She did, hard, knowing he loved it.

They rocked in the massive bed, tangling themselves in the sheets. Thousands of kisses, hundreds of deep strokes later, Aerin felt the soft sweet oblivion of her climax swim over her in a wet, pulsing, swelling wave.

She barely felt his teeth sink into her. Barely felt him drain her of blood, nearly to the point of death. But she tasted his blood as he slashed a line across his chest and let it flow into her open, waiting mouth. It was sweet and it was hot and it filled her like sunlight, burning her from the crown of her head to the very tips of her toes.

The scalding splash of his ejaculate filled her, burned her, and still he thrust and thrust and thrust. She came again and died her mortal death in his sheltering embrace. Darkness took her, and still Violanti was joined with her, rocking inside of her. Taking her down into the shadows of her death with a smile on her face.

It was three days before she awakened again. Born to the blood, stronger than she'd ever been. And Violanti was there, deep in her body, bringing her climax after climax. Loving her. Keeping her safe. In those three long days and nights he hadn't left her. Not once.

He vowed to her and to himself that he never would, not ever again.

Epilogue

Aerin's mouth moved over his cock, savoring the magically sweet taste of his come. It always surprised her, this sweet taste, a mixture of semen and blood and magic. She loved it. She loved everything about him.

"I can't. No more. You're driving me crazy, woman! That's three times already. You've drained me dry, I've no more to give."

Her gaze rose to meet his, dubious and disbelieving. Her mouth worked over him and she let him see her efforts, knowing it would make him crazy with lust.

It did. Quickly. His cock swelled bigger in her mouth, nearly choking her. He thrashed. "Untie me so that I can fuck you properly, you minx."

Laughing, she released his cock with a loud, wet smack. She reached up to the leather bonds that held him, knowing full well that he had the strength to break them, but loving him for the iron will of his restraint in not doing so. He'd promised not to cheat tonight. He'd promised to lie there in the black room, bound and trapped, while she had her wicked way with him. He'd kept his word.

No sooner had the last tie loosened than she was flung onto her back, Violanti's body covering hers heavily. With one long, smooth thrust he was seated to the hilt inside her welcoming warmth.

"So sweet, love, so fucking sweet," he said, his accent thick and lilting in her ear.

Aerin bit his shoulder, drawing blood with her fangs. Violanti roared his pleasure and returned the favor. They bit and clawed at each other, the tiny exquisite pains of their wounds heightening their arousal. Soon they were covered in a light sheen of blood and sweat, rolling about on the floor.

Violanti rose up out of her, then thrust violently back into the depths of her body, his balls slapping heavily against her anus, his cock reaching so far into her she thought she might choke. The force of his thrusts was so strong she knew it would have shattered the bones of any human. But she was lucky enough to no longer be human and she met the force of his thrusts with her own considerable strength.

She rolled with him and he let her, straddling him, taking him deep. His hands dug into the cushion of her hips, guiding her. "I don't believe it," he said in shock, seconds before he filled her with his come.

His shout made the walls vibrate.

Aerin bounced and rode, hanging on and enjoying the ride as he thrashed beneath her in the throes of a violent orgasm. He thrust particularly hard into her, slamming her down with his hands at her hips as he did, and she followed him into ecstasy, screaming her own surprise and exhilaration to the ceiling.

They collapsed in a heap upon the bed.

"Not bad for our fiftieth anniversary, wouldn't you say sugar girl?"

Aerin laughed. And promptly crawled back atop him, just to make sure there was no question.

The following excerpt from "Ravenous-The Horde Wars", © Sherri L. King, 2003 is available in e-book at www.ellorascave.com and coming soon in paperback.

RAVENOUS

Sherri L. King

Prologue

"Die, you son of a bitch—*hijo de puta*. Die! God, why won't you just die?" Cady Swann choked out as she buried her hands in the gushing black fount of the demon's chest. She searched out the giant beating heart of the beast, seeking to crush it and end the struggle at last. Her hands closed around the slippery black organ and she sunk her fingers deep.

"*Die!*" The demon's clawed hands were digging into the flesh of her back, as the monster tried to make her join him in the throes of death. Cady's hands tore into the burning, putrid heart of the monster, sinking into flesh and sinew as if they were an over-ripe orange. Dark, sticky blood erupted from where her hands were buried, drenching the both of them as they struggled.

Bracing herself against the flailing form of her dying foe, she jerked back, away from the grasping claws at her back, and away from the open cavity of the creature's chest. Stumbling, she broke free at last of the creature's embrace, its black, oozing heart still clutched desperately in her fists. The skin of her back was aflame. It was an accompanying pain for the myriad other bruises she had sustained during the night's dark work.

Ignoring her wounded body's weakened condition, she immediately set to work on the still-pulsing organ in her grasp. She pulled upon the humming power that even now flowed like a raging torrent through her form, drawing upon the supernatural strength that she would need in order to fulfill her task.

With a strength that would have torn the limbs from a mere mortal man, she ripped the preternatural heart in two. The wet, tearing sound of it echoed through the moonlit wood. Pulling a small container of lighter fluid from her pocket, she doused the hideous heart, lit a match and set it ablaze.

The fallen form of her monstrous foe writhed and screamed as its heart was swallowed in the flames. Moments later with a gurgling, choking sound the creature was still at last. Dead without its beating heart.

She'd learned the hard way that to leave even a small bit of the heart still unburned would give the creature a chance to rise from its death. So it was after the heart had been reduced to a blackened husk of ash that she rose wearily from her crouch on the forest floor. With tired eyes she surveyed the scene around her.

Her night vision was excellent thanks to her 'spooky talents' — a phrase she liked to use when referring to her enhanced senses. She could clearly see the fallen forms of two of the monsters as they lay dead about her. She would need to burn the bodies, she knew, to wipe away all traces of their existence. To hide the evidence of their evil.

No one must know these beasts existed. No one.

The two monsters she'd just killed brought the night's score up to five. And she still had four hours before dawn in which to find more of them to kill. She could feel the presence of more monsters out in the night. It was like an electric hum in her blood. Wearily she released a long-suffering sigh.

It was going to be a long night.

Chapter One

Her hands were covered in the black muck of demonic blood. Her clothes were saturated in the thick, viscous substance, causing the fibers to harden and stick to her skin like glue. The job was getting more and more dangerous as time went on. If job it could be called, this strange nightlife she lived.

Unfortunately, if killing these monsters — vicious beings with preternatural strength and power — was a job, it sure didn't pay anything. Nor was it a career that promised much hope in the way of comfortable retirement. Hell, it was highly doubtful she'd even live to see retirement.

No. Killing the evil, murderous monsters was not so much a job for her as it was a calling. She'd been doing this for fifteen years now. Saving her town, maybe the world, from demonic infestation. Though admittedly she'd battled more and more often in recent months. This was her life.

One thing was certain. She had no intention of slacking off in her self-appointed duties any time soon.

As far as she knew the threat was limited to her hometown of Lula, Georgia. And for certain she was the only person who knew of the monsters' existence. Whether these creatures were an invading force of evil minions sent from hell to invade the world, or simply abominations who'd come to her town by chance, she didn't know. But no matter the answers to her endless questions, she had to fight the creatures. Or hundreds, perhaps thousands, of lives would be put at risk.

It was a thankless job, but she couldn't, in good conscience, shirk her duties. Lula might be a small, out-of-the-way railroad town, but it was her home. She cared about the simple, country-bred citizens. Knew most of them quite well. It was up to her to keep them safe.

Cady entered the darkened foyer of her small home situated on the outskirts of town. Her house was a humble one. Hardly the type of place you'd think a supernatural assassin would call home. The plain-fronted farmhouse had been built by her great-grandfather, and had been bequeathed to Cady in her grandmother's will upon her death, three years before.

She loved this house. It was her only safe haven.

It was a structure rich with fond memories. Memories of quiet summer days that smelled of sun-warmed crops growing in the garden. Of dancing in soft evening rain, and of tobacco-smoke from her grandfather's ever-burning pipe.

Her grandparents had raised her here after the death of her family, in the comforting shelter of their quiet home. She missed them both desperately. Her grandfather had died of a stroke when she was eighteen and her grandmother had died in her sleep nine years afterward.

She'd had many good years with her grandparents, true, but she still missed them with an aching heart. It was hard to be alone in so frightening and dangerous a world. Hard to acknowledge the fact that no one was waiting for her when she came home.

Cady breathed out a heavy sigh. Knowing that her memories would not leave her in peace this night, she leaned against the doorframe and looked into the darkness of her home.

She wondered, not for the first time, if this was all there was to life. *Her* life. Fighting almost nightly to save the innocent, then coming home alone to an empty house. Struggling to stay afloat financially and mentally. Only to have to do it all over again the next night.

She wondered if the monsters would suddenly stop coming. Maybe just as suddenly as they had first come that stormy night fifteen years ago. The night they'd killed her parents and little brother, Armand. The night she'd left her childhood behind and taken up the chase as if a gauntlet had been thrown, forever dedicating her life to the pursuit and destruction of the monsters.

Cady jerked back to herself. She had no time for such frivolous reveries. What she needed was a bath and a cup of hot, soothing tea. The sky outside was starting to lighten as the sun rose to bring the dawn. The monsters could not move about by day, so she and the people of Lula were safe…until the next nightfall. And the next. And the next.

* * * * *

Shoulders slumped and achy, Cady stepped further into the room. Even though the sky outside was brightening, little of the illumination reached beyond the windows of her home. Deep shadows swallowed the interior of the house but Cady didn't bother switching on a lamp to light her way. She was simply too tired to bother and too in need of a hot shower to waste the time.

It was a mistake. One she was not soon to forget.

From deep within the shadows, an arm struck out and wrapped itself around her neck. With a choked gasp, Cady struck out at the large form behind her. Satisfaction flooded her when she connected a solid blow against her attacker's head. She wasted no time, and brought her booted foot solidly against the instep of her assailant. As she heard the pained grunt from the form behind her, she thrust her elbow into a firm, muscled midriff and tried to squirm free of the restraining arm around her throat.

Instead of loosening his arm, her assailant tightened his chokehold on her, and brought his other arm around her middle. A large hand splayed wide across her stomach to better hold her still. She was jerked forcefully back against a hard muscled body. Her struggles were ignored, much like the buzzing of an insect.

The arm that encircled her throat suddenly contorted. Before her wide, startled eyes a glowing, blue-white blade erupted from the skin of her assailant's forearm. The electric glow illuminated most of the room. The blade arched out in a wicked curve from the muscular arm, to rest the deadly, winking point just below her chin.

"Do not move if you wish to live, *human*," a voice growled deeply into her ear.

Cady ceased her struggles abruptly—not because she feared that the man behind her would end her life—but because his voice compelled her to do his bidding. His voice was deep, but melodiously pure in tone, like the voice of an archangel. She suddenly had no will to struggle against him. In those heartbeats that followed the command of his magical voice she would have been willing to do anything for him.

Anything at all.

"With whom do you swear allegiance, mortal? Daemon or Shikar?"

"What do you mean?" she rasped out.

"Are you friend to the Shikar Alliance or to the Daemon Horde? Answer me, woman. Now, or I will bleed you out where you stand. You will be dead before you hit the floor."

"I swear I have no idea what you're talking about. And even if I did, why should I tell you? I mean—we haven't even been properly introduced," she quipped, before mentally cursing her smart-assed mouth. It was always getting her in trouble.

Fuck it. She was already in trouble.

Suddenly the hands that held her cruelly, roughly against her captor's hard form, released her. She was spun roughly around, then pinned once more so that she faced him in the shadows. The arm sporting the wicked magical blade rested across her clavicle, once again placing the deadly point against her chin.

Cady's dark eyes flew up to the face of her captor, only to find it hidden in shadows too deep for her night vision to penetrate. Not even the bright glow of the blade at her throat pierced the shadows that swallowed her attacker's features. It was as if he controlled where the light fell, and he had no wish to reveal himself to her.

The hand that rested hot and firm upon her back, holding her tight against him, dug cruelly into the claw-wounds at her back. It made her wince and fight against the urge to cry out. She felt the commingled ooze of her congealed blood and that of the monsters she'd killed squish between her back and his splayed hand.

"You have the Daemons' foul stench upon you, but you are virtually unharmed. How do you explain this, human? Do you dare consort with the Horde? Are you the

Daemons' concubine, a wanton follower of their evil ways?" His fingers dug more forcefully into the wounded flesh of her back.

Cady's vision grayed as pain wracked her battle-weary body. She gritted her teeth against a scream but could not hold back an agonized gasp. She rallied her last reserves of strength and braced herself to fight. Her pain, fear and anger fueled the fires of her attack.

Taking her captor unaware, she swept her foot out and brought them both tumbling to the floor. Cady landed on top of him with a grunt. Wasting no time, she stabbed her hands into the exposed flesh of his throat, only to slam them with bruising force into the hardwood floor as he dodged her blow.

Using his substantially greater mass he turned them so that he towered over her as they struggled. But Cady was in full battle mode and it did not subdue her in the least. Using her knees, she kicked out against him, sending him flying over her head. Grabbing a dagger that she kept sheathed at her booted ankle, she whirled around to tackle her assailant as he struggled up from his position on the floor.

The man managed to shake her loose. Enough to stagger to his feet, at least. With mindless abandon she launched herself onto his back, sinking her teeth into his shoulder. She hung on for dear life as he tried to pry her off of him once more. Growling around the mouthful of flesh and muscle in her gripping jaws, she brought the knife to bear and sank it deep into his side. Hot wet blood spilled out over her hand before she was flung across the room. She had enough sense to brace herself for the impact that was sure to come—only to find herself suddenly plucked from her wild flight in the air by a hand encircling her throat.

He moved so fast! Faster than she could ever move, and she was an enhanced human. Or so she liked to think.

Her nails clawed the hand at her throat, leaving deep, weeping furrows behind. With a menacing growl her assailant brought her back against a wall. Her entire body was held inches above the floor by just the one hand clamped around her throat. Cady still could not see his face, but now she could see his eyes.

They were the same eyes she looked into each time she killed one of the monsters. His eyes were yellow-gold, with bold red rings around the pupils and irises. Though admittedly his eyes were clearer, lacking the bloodshot, glazed look that the monsters sported. In fact, they glittered like translucent jewels from beneath the longest, darkest lashes she'd ever seen.

This man was clearly different from a monster. His skin wasn't blistered and slimy, his blood appeared to be red instead of inky black, and he spoke plainly in English so that she could understand him. His voice was far too beautiful to belong to a monster. But his eyes were irrefutably alien and so like the monsters' that she wondered if he were a new breed of the hideous beings.

The thought left her cold and full of terror. If there were more enemies like the one she now faced, she feared she would never live to see another dawn.

In hopeless desperation Cady reached out before her, seeking out the soft, vulnerable flesh that shielded his heart. In her experience, every monster she'd ever faced had each possessed the same mortal weakness. The flesh of their chest cavities was like soft, over-ripe peaches, easily torn asunder to lay bare their hideous hearts. Her legs flailed over the empty space between them and the floor. With brutal force she struck out at his chest.

Only to bruise her knuckles against the hard, firm muscles that shielded his heart.

Oh God, she thought. *What is he?*

The assailant shoved her more forcefully against the wall, striking her head cruelly against it. Even as her vision dimmed from the blow to her skull she refused to cease her struggles. This must have angered him, because he raised his free hand and slowly brought a single finger to rest against her shoulder.

"Don't make me hurt you, woman. Cease your fight, and answer my questions; the dawn is almost upon us."

"*Fuck you*," she choked out, lashing out with her fist. She aimed for his nose, but he managed to evade her blow so that it glanced off of his cheekbone instead. Regardless, she felt no small amount of satisfaction knowing that he would at least bear a bruise for her efforts.

"I'm not really in the mood, just now," his beautiful voice bit out, just before a blue-white blade shot out from the tip of his finger. It stabbed cleanly through the muscle of her shoulder, like a hot knife through butter.

Cady screamed as the searing pain in her shoulder registered to her brain. Her assailant loosened his hold so that the weight of her body rested on the blade that ran straight through her shoulder and beyond into the wall behind her. She was suspended on that keen and wicked pain as he bent forward to breathe softly into her face.

"Do not make me hurt you further, little one." Was his voice gentler? Did she detect some small regret at his cruelty staining the dulcet tones of his voice? Or was she so consumed by pain that she was imagining things?

"Answer my questions, and your suffering will end. Are you friend or foe to the Shikars? Speak the truth or I will know you lie."

"I...I...it *hurts*," she whimpered. She could not think beyond the pain of the bright blade that pierced her flesh. Later, probably, her show of weakness would shame her. But not now. Now she wanted nothing but to escape from the horrible pain.

"I know it hurts, but you would not cease your struggles. I did not intend to come here and visit harm upon you. I merely wanted answers—answers which you still have yet to give me." His last words were gritted out and he twisted his finger, causing the blade to bite more cruelly into her tender flesh.

"God! Please!" she screamed as the pain unbelievably intensified. "I'll tell you anything—*anything*! Just...*just stop*."

"With whom do you side? Shikar or Daemon?"

"I—I don't know any Shikar or Daemon," she managed. It surprised her that she could talk at all. Her body had begun to shake and tremble with the waves of agony.

"You speak the truth...and yet you do not. You smell of the Daemons. You are covered in their filth." His intense, burning eyes blazed a trail down her form.

"You mean the monsters?" Her thoughts were a jumble, but she managed that bit of reasoning before she once more gave in to the pain that drove her. She moaned and writhed against the blade in her shoulder, seeking to keep her weight from bearing down so heavily upon it.

She braced herself by holding onto his wrists with both hands. He certainly was strong. His arm didn't even tremble under her weight. Their breath met between them — his deep and calm, hers shallow and rapid. He brought his free hand up to lay it softly over hers. She wondered if he meant his gesture to be comforting. Oddly enough, it did serve to comfort her a little...until another wave of pain swept her up once more.

"Daemons, monsters, hell-spawn — they are the things whose blood now soak your clothing," he breathed deeply as if scenting some fragrant perfume on the wind, "as well as your own."

"I killed seven of them tonight." Her voice shook with the effort of biting back her cries of pain. "I'll kill you as well and break even with my record of eight...just give me a second to catch my breath, okay?" She knew her boasting words were foolhardy in the extreme, but she couldn't help it. More than the pain, she hated being at his mercy, and the only way she could lash out was with words.

"Such brave boasts from so small a mortal woman. So you are no friend to the Daemons. You've met them in battle and triumphed. But you are a woman, not a Shikar warrior. How can this be? I sense the truth of your words, but how is it possible? You are...*human*," he spat out the last word as if it were some vile epithet.

"It hurts...hurts so bad," she whispered weakly. She could no longer focus on his words, but she was far beyond caring. Her head was swimming, her brain going fuzzy. She hated her weakness, but she'd never felt such an invasive pain before. In all her years of battling against the forces of evil she'd never before sustained such a debilitating and painful injury.

"I will leave for now. The dawn has arrived. But I will be back—and we will talk. You have caught the attention of my people, and we will have the answers we seek from you." He pulled the blade from her shoulder, catching her to him as she fell.

"Until we meet again, woman." He breathed the words at her ear, making them a promise. A threat.

Her world became darkness, as she fell into a swoon to escape the pain.

About the author:

Sherri L. King lives in the American Mid-West with her husband, artist and illustrator Darrell King. Critically acclaimed author of *The Horde Wars* and *Moon Lust* series, her primary interests lie in the world of action packed paranormals, though she's been known to dabble in several other genres as time permits.

Sherri L. King welcomes mail from readers. You can write to her c/o Ellora's Cave Publishing at P.O. Box 787, Hudson, Ohio 44236-0787.

Why an electronic book?

We live in the Information Age—an exciting time in the history of human civilization in which technology rules supreme and continues to progress in leaps and bounds every minute of every hour of every day. For a multitude of reasons, more and more avid literary fans are opting to purchase e-books instead of paperbacks. The question to those not yet initiated to the world of electronic reading is simply: *why?*

1. *Price.* An electronic title at Ellora's Cave Publishing runs anywhere from 40-75% less than the cover price of the <u>exact same title</u> in paperback format. Why? Cold mathematics. It is less expensive to publish an e-book than it is to publish a paperback, so the savings are passed along to the consumer.

2. *Space.* Running out of room to house your paperback books? That is one worry you will never have with electronic novels. For a low one-time cost, you can purchase a handheld computer designed specifically for e-reading purposes. Many e-readers are larger than the average handheld, giving you plenty of screen room. Better yet, hundreds of titles can be stored within your new library—a single microchip. (Please note that Ellora's Cave does not endorse any specific brands. You can check our website at www.ellorascave.com for customer recommendations we make available to new consumers.)

3. *Mobility*. Because your new library now consists of only a microchip, your entire cache of books can be taken with you wherever you go.

4. *Personal preferences are accounted for.* Are the words you are currently reading too small? Too large? Too...**ANNOYING**? Paperback books cannot be modified according to personal preferences, but e-books can.

5. *Innovation*. The way you read a book is not the only advancement the Information Age has gifted the literary community with. There is also the factor of what you can read. Ellora's Cave Publishing will be introducing a new line of interactive titles that are available in e-book format only.

6. *Instant gratification.* Is it the middle of the night and all the bookstores are closed? Are you tired of waiting days—sometimes weeks—for online and offline bookstores to ship the novels you bought? Ellora's Cave Publishing sells instantaneous downloads 24 hours a day, 7 days a week, 365 days a year. Our e-book delivery system is 100% automated, meaning your order is filled as soon as you pay for it.

Those are a few of the top reasons why electronic novels are displacing paperbacks for many an avid reader. As always, Ellora's Cave Publishing welcomes your questions and comments. We invite you to email us at service@ellorascave.com or write to us directly at: P.O. Box 787, Hudson, Ohio 44236-0787.